COWBOY
GHOST

Also by
Robert Newton Peck

COWBOY GHOST

Robert Newton Peck
Author of *A Day No Pigs Would Die*

■ HarperCollins*Publishers*

Library of Congress Cataloging-in-Publication Data

Peck, Robert Newton.

Cowboy ghost / Robert Newton Peck.

p.   cm.

Summary: Growing up without a mother and with an aloof father on a cattle ranch in
Florida in the first part of the 1900s has made Titus very close to his older brother, Micah,
and determined to make Micah proud of him when the two go on their first cattle drive
together.

ISBN 0-06-028168-5. — ISBN 0-06-028211-8 (lib. bdg.)

[1. Cowboys—Fiction.   2. Brothers—Fiction.   3. Fathers and sons—Fiction.
4. Florida—Fiction.]   I. Title.

PZ7.P339Co   1999   98-34915

[Fic]—dc21   CIP

                                                                        AC

Typography by Matt Adamec

3   4   5   6   7   8   9   10

❖

First Edition

The American cowboy originated in Florida.
Centuries before there ever was a Texas,
cowhands pushed horses, cattle, and wagons
across Florida flats, battling Seminoles,
heat, or hurricanes.
To several cowfolks I owe thanks for being
my friends, neighbors, and teachers:

Mex Cruz
Rusty Ragland
Hank Redpath
Charlie No Land
Miss Alpa Mae Mixter
And my horse partner,
Bill Ten Hoopen.

Without them, there would be no Cowboy Ghost.
—*Robert Newton Peck*

COWBOY
GHOST

*"Ain't nothing like the excite of
riding a strong horse onto fresh turf.
Ground that's never been hoofed.
A man's gotta fork across uncustom
land to discover his own self."*

Vinegar

PROLOGUE

✕☐

I t was Sunday.

Early that morning, we hitched a mare to the one-seater buckboard. Mrs. Krickitt, our housekeeper, drove the two of us into town, the eleven miles to Dry Bone.

Of all the people on Spur Box, our Florida cattle ranch, Mrs. Krickitt was the only woman, and I was the only little boy. We were also the only churchgoers. Mrs. Krickitt had explained why: Sunday morning crowded a Saturday night, a time when my father, my growed-up brother, and most of our cowhands attended a Dry Bone establishment called The Bent Ace.

On Sunday they hosted headaches.

As I sat properly erect on the buckboard's hard wooden seat beside our housekeeper, my hair was slicked, parted, and reeked of pomade. All due to Mrs.

Emma Krickitt's rigid requirement for a Sunday's stiff-bristle grooming. Had a horsefly lit upon my head, the poor critter would have slipped and sprained all six ankles.

"Today," she said, as Dolly's hoofs clopped into Dry Bone, "is a special Sunday. As you're now seven years old, you shall be awarded your very own Bible, with your name on it."

What she promised proved true.

Along with a dozen other squirmers and scratchers, I was presented a small black Holy Bible by our preacher. His name was Reverend Amos Throckfert Stonebreaker, the biggest Baptist I'd ever seen. And near to the biggest *anything*. To me, blinking up at his ruddy face and hog-barrel chest, Brother Amos looked far larger than merely one person. More like a congregation.

"God loves you," he intoned upon us from above, like thunder from Mount Sinai, drenching me with a few unfamiliar scraps of Scripture, plus his personal blessing. We then prayed. "Amen," he rumbled, severing the direct connection between Heaven and Dry Bone.

Leaving town, with the eager ears of our mare leaning forward toward home, I proudly sat West Point straight, my new Bible firmly clenched in both hands. I'd been warned not to drop it. Mrs. Krickitt's prediction had been on target. Sure enough, my name was inside, along with strangers like Solomon and Noah; and Numbers, whom I figured were baseballers in uniform.

Again I cracked it open to steal a peek. There, boldly and blackly printed, was inscribed my name and also the year of my birth:

Titus Timothy MacRobertson
1908–

Between the lofty pair of unpainted posts we rode. Above us arched the name of our ranch: SPUR BOX. And with it a wooden enlargement of our cattle brand: the six-pointed rowel wheel of a spur linked to a square box.

Away off to our right, some of our many cows were grazing. Beside almost every cow, a little white egret waited for a hoof to flush a bug. In the distance, beyond a thick stand of live oaks and pines, gray barns slowly loomed into view. Slightly above, on a knoll, our white house and its long front veranda, dotted with a row of white wicker chairs. Dolly's trot picked up a pace. Tightening on the long leather ribbons, our house-keeper's shiny dishwater fingers contained the mare's impatience, to keep her from breaking stride.

"Oh, this afternoon," Mrs. Krickitt moaned in a dry voice.

"Who do you suppose'll win?"

"Evil." She sighed. "On any weekday, it wouldn't tickle my interest. Or approval. But today, on a Sabbath Sunday, the upcoming event do seem a shoddy way to revere a day of righteous rest."

"Aren't you going to root for Micah?"

"More a pity than a cheering. I can't blame a mite of this contest on your brother. Micah's always been sweeter than honey, but the bees don't know it." As the lines on her face creased deeper, her voice sounded starchy. "I blame *him*."

I knew.

Not even for a heartbeat did I suspect that Mrs. Krickitt was talking about the stranger from Dry Bone, the one coming to Spur Box today to stand against Micah. Even though all week long I'd kept on hearing our cowhands mentioning his name.

Mr. Greer O'Ginty.

Whenever I was around, our hands usual stayed mum. However, I still picked up that he was strong, and tough. And mean. One night at The Bent Ace, this certain Mr. O'Ginty won almost a hundred bucks. How? By hefting a mule up off the floor. Two of our cowhands, Spout and Vinegar, had been present at The Bent Ace to see it. Yet even then, they couldn't quite believe it until realizing they'd each kissed good-bye a ranch-earned dollar. A whole precious day's pay.

"When this O'Ginty fights in the ring," Vinegar Swinton had told Domino, "they repute he's hiding a tiny round rock inside each fist."

"Is that truth?" I asked Mrs. Krickitt.

"Is what true, Titus? Speak up."

I mentioned what I'd heard off Vinegar, about the mule, and then about Mr. O'Ginty's fist of rocks. "Be it fair to do such?"

Mrs. Krickitt touched my hand. "Now, sometimes following a Saturday night in Dry Bone, old Vinegar Swinton tends to say more'n his prayers. So don't fret a fancy about it."

Right easy, Mrs. Krickitt gently guided Dolly beyond our grain shed and tackroom, coaxing her to back the buckboard into its comfortable slot under a slanted roof. As I jumped down, she whistled me to a halt.

"Tee . . ."

"Yes'm?"

"Were I you, I'd aim clear of the bunkhouse, least-wise for another hour. I figure you cotton to splendor your new Bible in front of the hands, even if you have to kick 'em conscious. Some you'll have to push thirty feet to start their hearts. Go careful. Show it only to those who can stand without crutches."

So I didn't visit the bunkers.

Instead, inside our main house, I tiptoed upstairs. The door to my father's room stood open. No sign. His tidy bed didn't look like it had cradled a sleeper. So I kept on going down the hall to my brother's. After pushing the door a few inches, I recognized that big familiar mound of manhood and muscle, a eighth of a ton, sagging his bed.

Seeing him made me smile. It always did, because Micah Samson MacRobertson was the finest twenty-year-old brother a kid could have or even dream of inheriting. Sometimes he'd read me a poem he wrote. Or sing me a song. Being his personal pest made me the luckiest kid in Florida.

When I'd started to talk, years ago, Mrs. Krickitt told me about the first word I ever spoke. It was a name.

Micah.

When I jumped on him, my brother appeared to be already awake. "Little buddy," he asked, "how was church?"

"Long. It lasted near a year. The sermon was about Sin, and as far as I could study, Reverend Stonebreaker was solid set against it." But instead of church, I was thinking about this afternoon, and Mr. Greer O'Ginty. So

I offered my brother some advice. "Micah, today when you fistfight, best you hide a little rock inside each hand."

"My, my, my," Micah said, mussing my hair. "There's a lot of gears grinding underneath all your frilly-smell pomade."

I recoiled. "Do I smell like a *lady?*"

Micah nodded. "But not a church lady. Closer to the Hell's Belles, the ladies from the second floor of The Bent Ace."

"What's up there?"

"Believe it or not, Tee, I never ventured up those red-carpet stairs. Only heard tell. From a few of our more *social* members of Spur Box."

"I guess you'd rather fistfight."

"No." He shook his big shaggy head. "Not hardly."

"Why do you do it?"

Micah sighed.

"Maybe," he said, "because Father used to box, long ago, and can't anymore." Touching my face with a huge hand, he smiled. "I fistfight so *you* won't ever git pressured into it."

Hearing him made me sad. So I decided that perhaps a change of subject might brighten him up.

"Looky here. At church I got a Bible."

With a grunt, Micah sat up in bed. "So you done."

He grinned. "Same way I received mine, thirteen years ago." Cracking my Bible open at about the middle, he said, "Let's you and me find what's inside."

"What is this story?" I asked.

"Isaiah."

"How come you picked it to look at?"

Without answering, he began to read in a soft Sunday voice. As he read, I noticed the two numbers on the Isaiah page. It said 48.

"*Because I knew,*" Micah read, "*that thou art obstinate, and thy neck is an iron sinew, and thy brow is brass.*"

He closed the Bible.

There were voices outside Micah's window. Someone pounding. *Whack. Whack. Whack.* Men were arguing about where something ought to be.

I looked out the window; men were malleting four stout posts into the sand. One man was giving orders. It was my father. Rob Roy MacRobertson. He had rarely spoke to me in seven years because he didn't seem to cotton to know me. Nor did I understand our mighty ox-backed senior of Spur Box.

"What are they doing, Micah?"

"Squaring off a ring, Titus, that's all. It's for this afternoon." He looked down at his scarred knuckles. "At three o'clock."

"What you readed to me from out of my new Bible, was that there hard brass and iron about Mr. O'Ginty? Is he the one?"

Slowly shaking his head, Micah silently stared out of his bedroom window . . . at Father.

SPUR BOX
1924

Nine years later . . .

CHAPTER ONE

icah tossed me a coiled rope.

"Tee," he told me, "shake out a loop. Seeing as today's your sixteenth birthday, Father is bound to start looking your way." His face sobered to serious. "And expecting."

In my fingers, a rope had seldom felt friendly. Only harsh and hairy. Yet I pulled a hoop, holding the double-back in my right hand, the main coil inside my left. I'd growed up around ropes. Seen 'em work. And heard many a straining lariat buzzing along fence wood.

"Face him, Tee."

A gray mustang and I were the only two beings with our feet on the ground. And inside. My brother and a dozen of our cowhandlers sat on the circular corral's top rail, pointing at me with ragged knees and the scuffed-up toes of their boots.

Instead of tack, the gray wore the disagreeable ear-back expression of a unbroke critter, a horse fixing to break a man.

"Stare his eyes," Micah said, "like you don't need a rope. As if you'd hanker to grab his head, gnaw his ear, and force him down to yielding."

For years, I had watched this stunt performed by Micah, by old Vinegar Swinton, probable our ablest hand, or by our foreman, Mr. Ornell Hopple. But never by me.

"Be his boss," Spider yelled. "Conquer that cusser."

Earlier, I'd suspected that today might be troubling. At breakfast, Mrs. Krickitt had warned that a bit of bother was up, about to snort my way. "Your initiation," she told me. "Be grateful that *himself* is out of town, at the Cattleman's Whoop-De-Doo in Naples, and won't be squinting his sullen silence at you. Or spitting, if you fail."

The gray was a new-growed mustang, a gypsy stud recent captured on our Spur Box range. And raw. Never yet knowed a saddle, bridle, or oats. Rangy. Ready to rid himself of me, a rope, or any human devil with the gumption to challenge his liberty or his stallionhood.

"Go him slow, Tee." It was my brother's steadying voice. "I done this when I turned sixteen. So can you."

My teeth clenched.

Didn't Micah know how sturdy he got built, and what a skinny bag of twigs I was? He'd always resembled the first six feet of an oak tree. A stout one. As massive a man as Father. Our neighbors usual remarked, "Micah is Rob Roy MacRobertson all over again."

But they were so wrong.

Right now, however, observations wouldn't be delivering me through today's baptismal. It had to be brains and bowels, pulling in tandem, like our yoke of Holstein oxen.

"Eye down the horse," I told myself. Make it a will of master over beast. All my life, I'd heard this wisp of wisdom around the bunkhouse, often sung to the wailing wheeze of Bug Eye's harmonica. Before I could talk (Mrs. Krickitt had informed me), Vinegar Swinton had stuffed a rope in my fingers. Spout had planted my butt to the back of a horse. And later, Hoofrot had showed me how to fasten a slipknot, or a belly cincher.

Now they were all watching, ready to root for me because I was a MacRobertson, and Spur Box was home. Their only children had been Micah and me.

"Soft now," Micah was saying. "Don't be hurrying at him. Just let that sunfisher know who's a raw and who's a rider."

Could I do it?

A simple chore, accomplished every workday morning six times a week by a ranch hand. Before it's even daybreak, he has to rope an unwilling horse, an animal half wild, a stringer hostile to punch work. All of the men now watching, except for Micah, began every sweating wage day with a primal act.

Now, it was my turn.

The mustang stood his ground inside the roomy corral, noticing my slow advance, seeming not impressed by a gangle of a lad who weighed half the heft of his bull of a brother.

As the gray snorted, I said, "Easy," trying to sound the smooth way Mr. Ornell Hopple, our ramrod, always sounded to me. Like he gargled with cream. Mr. Hop was a small man, weighing only a few pounds more than I did. Short. Slight of build and body. Eyes of gentle blue, the benevolent color you find in small patches on a very old bedroom quilt. Yet he was certain a top hand.

Wearing no iron and raising a unshod hoof, the gray broomtail pawed Florida, creating dark holes to freckle the surrounding sunbaked tan of the sand.

"Horse," I said, "my name is Titus Timothy MacRobertson, and my family owns the land you're standing on. What's more, I'm fixing to roll a hoop on that handsome head of yours. Know why? Because you can't do a dang thing about it."

Advancing on the gray, I could hear what Spider had lectured me. "Don't swing a lasso to a animal unless need be. Waste of energy. Oh, and never hasten. Mosey. Ya saunter at a horse, close as courting, and then, if you git comfortable lucky, you might ease a noose over his ornery head."

"What happens next?" I'd asked.

"Next?" Hacking out a laugh, Spider scratched his six-foot-six person. "Next, once he awares a rope to his gullet, you git your unlucky ass prepared to visit Hell."

In front of me stood a four-legged Satan, raw and red eyed, a unbroke outlaw who didn't plan to leg it lenient with even my father, Mr. Mac. However, with almost everyone on Spur Box creasing their Sunday butts on the upper rail (except for Father and Mrs. Krickitt), I wouldn't back off or hightail run. It was time to swallow my dose of dismal.

A second after the stallion lowered his head, then tossed it high again, I whipped my rope at him. Not so unlucky a throw. The loop circled fat, floated, then settled around the gray's neck. Neither of us knew quite what to do next.

"Yahoo!" one of our cowhands honked

It certain did not help.

A breath later, the horse took it in his miserable head that maybe something sorry was about to descend on him. And he'd better rear up on his hindquarters, nicker his panic, then strike the sunshine with both of his front hoofs flailing. Nostrils flaring, the mustang's eyes bulged as though to say, "If you want a piece of my meat, sonny, you're dang about to earn it."

Spider was right.

Suddenly I wasn't visiting Heaven. Unless, of course, Heaven is being jerked prone and your face plowing up inches of gritty topsoil, much of which is dried manure.

"Let go the rope, Tee!" a voice advised.

No! I wouldn't. Not even if this hellion of a horse dragged me brisket to breakfast. My fingers locked to the rope shaft and burned like a fire. Inside our corral, there was probable no single lick of land that my chin didn't plow up or swim through. That horse could certain canter and cover ground. Around we circled: he up and I down. But I didn't let loose my purchase on the rope. I couldn't. My fingers cramped into a grip.

Hearing the mustang grunting and breathing heavy convinced me he was tiring. So was I. Yet I hung on hard. Besides the panting of the pony, I also heard the yips, yelps, and Rebel yells from our Spur Box outfit. Maybe this clinched the critter closer to exhaustion. Only one fact mattered.

He quit a second before I did.

Near me, as I was lying in the dusty dirt of the corral, there was a spent beast leaning his flank to wooden rails, and wheezing. Crawling to him, then standing, passing my end of the rope around an upright post, I grabbed his steaming head, pretending to bite his ear.

A blast of approval roared out of every throat, as I got evaluated by respectful eyes. Men of experience. Were these hoots good or bad? Their racket prodded me into questioning who'd actual won. Because our Spur Box rowdies, when tanked, might even cheer a drunk throwing up.

"You took him, Tee," Micah whooped. "Bless the golly, my baby bro certain is a genuine MacRobertson."

CHAPTER TWO

Hold still," Mrs. Krickitt commanded.
Sitting on a hard kitchen chair, noticing her
needle and a long length of boiled white thread,
I informed her that I wouldn't require any of her stitches.

"Hush. You need more sewing than the stuffed-up
butts of ten Christmas turkeys. If you leave those bleeding gashes open to the weather around a barn and all
its flies, you'll possible infect yourself sicker than a
Saturday night."

"Your doggone iodine hurt bad enough."

Mrs. Krickitt grunted. "Well, do not cogitate it, Titus.
Because the iodine wounded the germs a whole bunch
badder."

With grinding molars, I took a couple dozen of her
merciless stitches. My eyes watered. Yet I wasn't actual

sobbing. Here on Spur Box, crying over anything wasn't permitted, as it'd be considered unmanly by Mr. Mac.

All of her stitching had, thus far, speared above my waist. Arms, chest, and shoulders. But then Mrs. Krickitt employed her scissors again, beginning to cut away my jeans, as she had earlier removed my tattered shirt, tore to a rag.

"Snake off your belt, Tee."

"Nohow. All due respect, I'm certain not going to expose my personal self *half naked* in front of *you*."

She grunted again. "Well now, sixteen year ago, you happened to be *entire naked*, on the night I attended your birthing. The mighty *himself* paced and paraded outside her bedroom door, yelling useless instruction." Mrs. Krickitt paused. Then, in a milder tone, said, "Your mother died. I couldn't save her."

Wanting to touch Mrs. Krickitt's hard hand, I resisted. Spur Box was hardly a home where anyone touched anybody else.

Except fisting in a ring.

In sixteen years, what little I'd learned about my mother, Eudora Mae MacRobertson, almost entire had come from our housekeeper. Micah rarely spoke about her because, I reasoned, it pained him too much. He bottled it up inside.

Nobody understood his hurting but Mrs. Krickitt and me.

Mother died when Micah was thirteen.

Until then, Mrs. Krickitt told me, he'd been a carefree child. "He was a hoot and a holler," she'd claimed more than once. "But her death turned him sober. Not sour."

Father, I felt, always resented me. Not that he ever honestly blurted it out. There were, however, those wordless moments when Rob Roy would glare at me, as though barely containing some deep-rooted urge to shout at me . . . "Your birth killed my beloved Eudora." Perhaps, in my father's mind, an additional child was unnecessary. He already had Micah, a boomer of a boy, to hammer and twist and warp into a second Rob Roy MacRobertson. A fistfighter. Another boxer with spurs.

"Stretch out," Mrs. Krickitt ordered.

Grimacing, I obeyed, lying belly down on our long kitchen table, on which we MacRobertsons took breakfast, apart from the black iron giant of a cookstove, the six-griddle Acme American where Mrs. Krickitt prepared so many of our meals.

"That ornery outlaw of a horse near about peeled you like a potato. Amazing you're still breathing."

Actual, I was holding my breath every time her cussed needle punctured my flesh, and also when the thread pulled tight.

"You about finished?"

"Mind your business," she snapped. "For thirty-five year, these needles of mine pierced and patched and pieced a regiment of ranch hands together. Those that got ripped at honest work. And, in the wee hours, more'n a few that aspired to become the toughest and dumbest drunk at The Bent Ace."

To prove her disapproval, our veteran housekeeper yanked a stitch a tug tighter than needed.

"Hey, go easy!" I yelped. "You aren't roping a broomtail. I'm Titus, in case you forgot. Can't admit I cotton to display a bare bottom in front of somebody of the female persuasion."

Bending, she whispered to my ear. "Who in Christendom do you think soaped that uppity behind of yours, when you were a wee babe? Then powdered your particulars with cornstarch? Before that, your big buffalo of a brother. Plus the embroidery I've pricked into ten score of bunk busters." She laughed. "All sections of their private anatomies. North and south."

"Is that so?" I knew it was.

Mrs. Krickitt nodded. "I've observed more naked

male flesh than a dozen of The Bent Ace hostesses. And," she huffed, "I can't favor of having been charmed by even a sacred square inch of the view."

It hurt me to laugh. As I did so, every stitch cried. But I wasn't about to challenge a housekeeper who sometimes had a temper that could spit upwind and bust a window.

Right then, Micah stuck a big curly head through the open doorway of the kitchen, then skinned off his cowboy hat. He did this for her, removing his headgear, in respect. Micah had always been her favorite. When he'd lost Mother, she'd been there to help replace the emptiness; to my brother, so much more'n a scrawny grayhaired lady who cleaned and cooked. Micah was a son she maybe ached for and never birthed. At age thirteen, when he'd been heartsick and busted apart, she glued him together.

"I heard hollering," he said. "How's Tee?"

"He'll repair," our housekeeper answered. "Can't say a likewise for either his shirt or his pants." She held up my blood-spattered garments for inspection. "He's a mess."

"Tee done honorable today," Micah said.

Before I could roll around in his praise, like a cat in sunshine, Mrs. Krickitt deposited her penny's worth: "All of this manhood madness is nothing more'n extra weight. Prove this. And prove that. You so-called gentle-men go lamebraining through life, wasting proof on all the other nitwits. You're all bona fide men. Accept it, relax, and smell a clump of clover."

Outside the kitchen, a sun had subsided and was tak-ing its rest. Or visiting the yonder edge of our world. When my eyes drooped, Mrs. Krickitt promptly directed me upstairs to bed. Micah stayed. While leaving the kitchen, I heard him pulling back a table chair to sit in. Following that, Mrs. Krickitt asked if'n he might notion a extra leftover slab of Georgia peach pie.

My usual starving brother said, "Sounds sublime."

Then the clatter of a fork, a plate upon the table, and maybe a mug of leftover coffee. Plus a few mumbled exchanges of guarded words.

Just as I started to climb the stairs, I overheard her say, "Micah, don't you allow it to happen. Please do not."

With a mouthful of pie, my brother hesitated with a slight grunt, then responded, "Above all else. I know. And you're right. Today was more a lesson for me than for Titus."

"Bless you, Micah. You savvy so much of this fam-ily, yet speak so little about it. Titus isn't burly like you, or Mr. Mac. What scares me almost to insanity is that it could turn so tragic if Tee tries to be." She sighed. "Out yonder in that horse corral, our youngster took it bloody dreadful. It could balloon, Micah, and you can't let it repeat."

"No," he said in a low voice. "One sacrificed son is ample. God help me, Mrs. Krickitt, I won't allow Father to eat him alive."

CHAPTER THREE

✗☐

I couldn't sleep.

The fires of iodine had burnt themselves out. My stitches, however, were still stinging worse'n a swarm of hot hornets, over my entire person, private and public.

"Enough of this," I groaned.

Creeping slowly off my bed, cautious not to disturb the slumbering of Mrs. Krickitt's knotted thread, I reached toward the floor for my boots. Stretching was torment. The boots, one at a time, got yanked over my bare feet. This took a spell. Not a speedy process. More like racing a snail.

Never, I'd been frequent warned since childhood, venture outside barefoot in a Florida night, to unmerciful stingers, fangs, and cactus.

Wearing only boots and purple-striped pajama pants,

I left my bedroom to tiptoe past Micah's crosscut snoring, easing mindful down the stairs. Then out the kitchen screen door to a sticky night. Wet. You could wring the air into a bucket. The sky was cloudy; no moon, and no stars. Just a misty moisture waiting to fall and rinse the cow dust off Florida; and coming up morning, make her shine.

Somewhere, off to the southwest, the sky flickered a few blinks. Many counts later, thunder rumbled a distant drum. Florida summer was relentless electricity.

I limped to the barn.

Unless the weather's a terror, our three Holstein milk cows reside outdoors, day or night, to keep the barn floor cleaner. Still and all, the barn was ripe from animals, sweaty harnesses, and grain. A good earthy smell. Dirt clean.

The barn was deserted. Except for one other member of Spur Box. Tail straight up, she padded toward me, more silent than a shadow.

"Well, good evening to you, Miss Cleo."

Strolling to me as unhurried as only a cat could be, Cleopatra arched her back and rubbed her head and flank against my right boot. Bending slow, I stretched down a hand to reward her friendship, until the stitches convinced me to remain rampant. Up straight.

"Sorry, your highness."

Closing her eyes, Cleopatra opened them again, at leisure, offering a catty communication in the only way she knew. And purring. I told her about today's gray mustang and how he most divided me into sections. The story, however, wasn't enough to hold her interest. Mice ventured out at night. And to a cat's sensitive nose (to anyone's), the aroma of a gray mouse beats the brown fragrance of stale iodine.

Once again, tail-high content, Miss Cleo wandered off at her own casual pace, going wherever a cat casually chooses to ramble.

The barn slept deathly quiet. Out on the meadow where the Holsteins were lying, a choir of crickets was holding a recital. Summoning all spirits of the night. But then, in one instant, every bug ceased its fiddling on command from a cricket captain of the guard.

In a breath, I suspected I wasn't alone!

With me in the barn, a presence, someone or something unknown and unseen. Perhaps whatever it was had no right to be around.

"Who's there?"

No answer came.

Only the black stillness of night, coming closer, and inching in. Something. But what? Who? Compelled to look behind me, I turned my head to stare at nothing except a large pair of open barn doors. Beyond, merely the expected black rectangle of night, lonely and lifeless. No intruder.

"Okay, I know you're there. Better speak up."

Hearing my own voice chilled me.

Then, with a forced grin beginning, I was reckoning that maybe Hoofrot or Fat Cat or Bagpipe, or any one of our cowhands, was hiding, trying to prank me into a panic.

Cold reason tapped my warm naked shoulder, as though to advise that, at twelve o'clock at night, there'd be precious few worked-out cowpokes with the energy left over to yahoo mischief. Not with breakfast five hours off.

"You are here. But I don't fear you. You're no gator, no bear, not a panther," I told it. "You are human. Or almost. Were you once alive, now dead, trying to invade me and live again?"

Something prodded me to speak a word, a name, one I'd never used in my entire life when addressing another person.

"Mother?"

How odd it felt to say.

So many countless times I'd longed to say "Mother," to the point of agony, because of Father. At the homes of my school chums, I'd heard all of them say the name of Mother or Ma or Mom. Or in jest, Maw. Hearing it used

ADMIT ONE

LITTLE TRAVERSE HISTORICAL SOCIETY

PRESENTS

Real Estate One

2016 HISTORIC HOME TOUR

SATURDAY, SEPTEMBER 24, 1 TO 4 PM

ADMIT ONE

ADMIT ONE

NO REFUNDS

Little Traverse Historical Society Home Tour

Convene at the Little Traverse History Museum at 1 pm
100 Depot Street

Tour Homes at:
102 Division Street ~ 816 Mitchell Street ~ 915 Waukazoo Street ~ 125
Bay View Avenue ~ 604 Bay Street ~ 218 Park Avenue in Downtown

RAIN OR SHINE

ADMIT ONE

in a shallow way made me writhe. Why did they bury their treasure? How, when they'd been given so much, did they insist on returning so little? At school, I actual overheard two girls complaining about certain parental restraints that cramped their social plans.

"It's so uppity," one gum chewer announced as she was repaving her vacant face in a purse mirror, "when our mothers talk back to us."

At that moment in school, had it been within my powers, I could easily have crated and shipped that hopeless girl to a Devil's Island leper colony. Or worse, to a brig of brats.

For me, Mother was a name I secretly whispered beneath the giant live oak tree, where a woman I never knew lay buried in Florida earth. As a sorrowful sentry, a crudely carved wooden marker stood above her grave, listing an inch or two to one side.

Eudora Mae MacRobertson
1869—1908

My mother wasn't here with me in the barn.

Someone else was.

Foolishly, I felt the pockets of my jeans for a wooden kitchen match. One striking flick of a thumbnail against a blue-and-white head would ignite a hurried hiss of sulphuric visibility. Then the mysterious other person might be located, lurking in a barn's shadows. Trouble is, I wasn't wearing any jeans. Only the lower half of pocketless pajamas. Fly open.

Looking down, I could see a torn place at my right knee, a rip that seemed to be begging for Mrs. Krickitt's needle.

"Sorry," I told my pajama pants. "Can't oblige you. Because all three hundred yards of her cussed boiled thread is now deposited in *me*."

Did I hear a laugh?

Inside my boots, my toes turned sudden cold.

"Mrs. Krickitt?"

Her name echoed off into the darksome, leaving me standing alone with a shabby opinion of myself. Of my fear. Too many times I'd run to her, wanting to kneel at her feet in our kitchen and bury my tearful face in her food-stained apron. Why? Because she was always *there*. Baking, scrubbing, absorbed in her disinfecting battle upon anything soiled, untidy, or disorderly.

Add to that unmannerly or improper.

Growing up, I had early decided that the Spur Box people were unevenly split into two teams. Mrs. Krickitt and Titus, the churchgoers, made up one team. The opposing forces mustered everyone else, with a possible exception of Micah, and maybe Ornell. My big brawny brother always seemed to stay impartial, an aloof referee, yet unaware of the companies of combatants.

Led by Father.

In childhood, I ran to Mrs. Krickitt with a skinned elbow. Later the injuries became internal. Invisible. Whenever my surly father spoke only at Micah, never to me, the bruises then inflicted couldn't be bandaged. My bleeding cut too deep.

"Micah."

Standing alone in the barn, saying his name, brought back the hope that someday I too might grow up to be massive. This, my approaching maturity slow taught me, wasn't to be. Reality established a toehold. A claim. What was that apt term Miss Witherspoon had used at school? Ah, it hit me. My brother and I were the *antithesis* of one another. Polar. He looked like Rob Roy. And as the poker hand lay dealt, faceup on the table, I was Eudora Mae.

Physically, my brother came from Father.

I from Mother.

This was no easy spoonful to swallow. Not for a lanky boy of sixteen, longing and lusting to become an adult. To prove out.

Did I hear somebody *spit*?

Impossible. Yet whenever a man cracks open a pocketknife, slices off a plug as Vinegar Swinton does, chews, and then hawks a brown stream of tobacco juice, the sound is commonplace. And quite familiar. There's no sound like it. Sort of the ratchety rattle as a shooter cocks a cartridge into the firing chamber of his eager rifle.

Waiting, I heard no more.

Yet an unknown presence seemed to be trying to contact me. One without a voice? It was a finger tap on my shoulder, perhaps to remind me of a fact I already knew. The something was definitely a human who'd weathered many seasons of Spur Box living. Not a warning. More like an omen, a prediction of the present based on the experience of the past.

Experience?

Three names came immediately to mind: Rob Roy MacRobertson, Vinegar Swinton, and our foreman, Ornell Hopple. Men who were half cow and half horse, Spur Boxers whose hearts and souls hung tight to our ranch, our home. Whoever he was, he was a cowhand, through and through.

But for now, only a Cowboy Ghost.

CHAPTER FOUR

Wondering if Father had returned from nearby Naples and might tune up trouble for missing me at the breakfast table, I pounced out of bed, reviving all my stitches. A hand flew to my mouth to muffle a tortured honk.

Pulling on a shirt and jeans, and secretly groaning the entire way down the stairs, I kicked myself to the kitchen. Only two people were present, thank the luck: Mrs. Krickitt (who was almost always there) and my brother. Fork in hand, knuckles up, mighty Micah was already attacking his seven eggs like they were still on the hoof and had to be butchered.

He looked up and grinned. "Good morning, Titus."

A yellow trickle of egg oozed down his chin. No problem. Micah's blue-gray work-shirt sleeve chased it and erased it.

"Hey, Micah." As I'd done since early childhood, I yanked back a chair next to my brother, warming a seat. "Good morning, Mrs. Krickitt."

"Morning, Tee." With a black skillet in her holder-protected hand, she half pivoted to recognize me. Her eyebrows raised. "Well, are you prospering?"

"Yes'm. A mite. Thanks for asking."

"Later, I'll want to gander a closer squint at your sewing, in case any of my fancy needlework begs another jab."

I winced. "Okay."

It would serve little purpose opposing her. Here on Spur Box, in matters pertaining to household management, family mealtime, and dedicated doctoring, our housekeeper's opinion got carved into granite or cast in bronze. Emma Krickitt needed no reminders about the boundaries of her awesome authority. On a cattle ranch, fences remained fences. She ranged beyond horizons. Nobody griped. Not my father, and certain not the lowliest most-recent-hired-on cowpoke. The lady, whenever she spoke her mind, was respected.

Beyond that. Revered.

We knew why. And, as our housekeeper served me a steaming plate of good-morning fortification with her customary "Eat up, Tee. It'll add beef to your bones," my mind reviewed what both Micah and

Mrs. Krickitt had told me true.

Even though she and my father had never ap-proached amity, when Mother died, Father requested Mrs. Krickitt to remain here at Spur Box. Pleaded with her. Perhaps knowing that Eudora Mae MacRobertson and Emma Krickitt had become more than a mistress and a cook.

They were friends. Like sisters.

Thus, she stayed.

"More grits, Micah?" she asked, hoping to please him.

"Oh, yes'm. Please."

After breakfast, Micah and I left the kitchen through the screen door, heading toward the barn. But I noticed my brother was shading his eyes, looking eastward into the morning sun. A rider was slow coming on a wore-out horse. The animal's head wasn't up and alert. Instead, it sagged low and lifeless. In the saddle, the rider's body seemed similar, as though both horse and rider were heading where they had no hanker to go, and too spent to get there.

They plodded closer.

"Drifter," I heard Micah mutter. "He might be just after a day's work, a day's dollar, and a full plate of grub. They come and go."

The stranger rode up to us and reined his weary

animal. The horse had three white-stocking legs. One brown. A bay, with a black mane and tail.

"Morning," Micah said.

As the man nodded, he seemed to stretch a fake smile at the pair of us, appearing as if he could employ a bath and a shave. He'd been chewing. So he leaned to one side an inch or two and spat. Itching to ask him if, by any chance, he visited our barn yesterday night, I held quiet. For some reason, I didn't think that a grubby stranger was my Cowboy Ghost.

"I'd be grateful of a job," the newcomer said. "Would your outfit take on another man?"

"Maybe," my brother told him. "But I'm not the person who hires. Better see our top hand, the foreman, Mr. Ornell Hopple. He handles all our hiring and firing."

"Where's he at?"

Gesturing at the building behind us, Micah said, "My guess, this time of day, he's most usual in his office. That's the private little room beside the bunks."

Without a word, the rider neck-reined his horse toward Mr. Hop's office at a slow gait.

"Before you enter," Micah warned, "*knock*. Mr. Hopple sometimes can bristle up when people don't do mannerly." We watched him leave us. "I got doubts," Micah said. "However, it's never been my say-so, or yours, who gets taken on here at Spur Box. And it's a wise rule, Tee. Father explained the *why* of it to me, a time ago. On this ranch, any hand who gits fired, for one reason or another, can't honest claim he got hisself axed by a MacRobertson."

"Makes sense."

"It really do." Micah poked me. "You know when Mr. Mac established that particular habit?"

"When?"

Resting a big boot on the bottom rail of the corral fence, Micah turned to me direct. "In 1893, right before he wed Mother. To protect his beloved Eudora from any revengeful cowpoke."

As we walked back toward the barn once again, Micah waited for me, realizing I was feeling sewed up stiffer than misery. Hobbling and hurting.

"You know," I told my brother, "that story is difficult to swallow. Not that I'm calling you a fibber, yet it's hard to believe that Mr. Rob Roy MacRobertson ever cared for anyone that much. Or at all."

"We dasn't ever rob him of her memory, Titus. Because when Mother died, a lot of him died with her."

CHAPTER FIVE

✕☐

Farley had quit.

Seems like his uncle in Georgia had been giving grief to his favorite relative, Aunt Edith, who'd raised him. So, after collecting his pay, Farley waved a so-long and headed north. And gone.

Ornell Hopple needed a man. So the stranger, who stated only that his name was Jilly, got hired on trial and ordered to go assist Domino.

With him, Jilly brung a saddlebag of nuisance.

"You never told me," he soon griped to Ornell, "I'd be working beside a African blacky." The big man sort of pointed a thick finger under Mr. Hop's chin, standing a step too close. "Or do nigger work."

Our foreman wasn't a man to be crowded by sass, or one to listen up shouting. Using his sweet-cream voice, he informed Jilly that Spur Box assessed men by their cowmanship, not their noise. And that it was Domino, not Jilly, who ought to feel insulted.

"On this here outfit," Hop told Jilly, "there ain't no nigger work, as you call it, or white work. It's plain toil. Best remember, seeing as you're the new kid in town."

"I ain't a kid."

Ornell softened his tone. "Then please quit behaving like one. Mr. Jilly, I know it's hot, dirty work. Cowhanding ain't never been bonnie as a night shift in Hell. That's our job, mister. Yours and mine. So you got yourself two choices. Tackle chores like a man, or lope off without supper."

Jilly pitched in.

Castrating the balls off bull calves, as well as branding our ⨉☐ into their kicking red hides, isn't a vacation. But Jilly proved himself able. Luckily for him, Domino respected anybody who could handle a frisky calf, plus a hot iron, so no more got mentioned.

At day's end, Jilly was natural invited to attack supper (along with all the other hands who'd rode in to wash up) at the bunkhouse mess tables.

Spur Box men ate well, thanks to Tin Pan.

He was our Chinese cook for the punchers. His name, he insisted in futility, was actual Pan Tin; but, as cowboys tend to nickname everything in sight, including

43

weeds, he got permanently tagged with Tin Pan. Ofttimes merely Tin.

Tin Pan cooked tasty and smiled frequent. Except for the times that his boss visited.

Mrs. Krickitt had hired him and daily inspected his kitchen and larder. Foodstuffs were her domain, a part of it, so she exercised her duties with commanding authority. Tin didn't confront her. Few did. During her inspections, he mumbled an incessant chant to express his displeasure. After all, he was a man. She merely a woman.

In China, there were no ladies like Emma Krickitt.

Micah and I often chuckled as a result of Tin's inadvertently teaching Mrs. Krickitt a few Chinese phrases, none complimentary, that debased an unfortunate listener's ancestry. Ironically, our housekeeper's English was consistently pure. However, whenever she checked on tidiness in the bunkhouse, she'd angrily release a few Asian expressions at whichever cowpoke was tracking in manure. Or sleeping in it. Her tirade, punctuated by Chinese profanity, was understood only by Tin Pan, who hooted in hilarity.

Their other common ground was flowers.

Tin favored gardening. Although he had few kind feelings toward Mrs. Krickitt, he made peace with her, planting tulips and marigolds by her back porch and also outside her kitchen window.

She noticed.

Such a pleasant gesture resulted in a truce and with Mrs. Krickitt's becoming the only person on Spur Box who called him by his preferred name: Pan Tin. This, whenever he bowed to her, made our little cook smile with his complete keyboard of eighty-eight teeth.

Hours earlier, Tin had been puttering among his variety of bloomage, but had unfortunately been observed by Jilly.

On his way in to supper, Jilly, because he'd been forbidden to berate Domino, decided to test his nasty against the cook. So, in his big boots, Jilly trampled through a row of Tin's pansy patch. And worse, called him Tin Pansy.

Tin, a third the size of Jilly, assaulted the big fellow with a cookstove temper and a steel spatula.

This altercation did nothing except to delay supper for a batch of gnaw-a-dog-hungry cowpunchers, all of whom accepted Tin Pan and his hearty meals. Without ceremony, four of the burliest hands grabbed Jilly and persuaded him by squatting on his face.

Dust finally settled and so did supper.

Bug Eye was torturing his harmonica; both coonhounds were fed and asleep. Cleopatra yawned, arose, stretched, and considered hunting for a slow mouse.

"Something's up down yonder," Mrs. Krickitt announced to Micah and me, tossing a pink-and-white-checkered dish towel over her shoulder. She looked beyond her kitchen window. "Trouble brewing on every griddle. I can smell it."

The odor arrived, in person, in the familiar form of Vinegar Swinton, elder statesman of the bunkhouse and frequent program chairman of a few horizontal refreshments (I don't mean billiards) at The Bent Ace.

"Miz Krickitt," he said through the screen door, holding a battered sweat-stained hat in one hand while scratching himself with the other, "some us waddies got the internal infernals. Kink knots." He almost blushed. "A misery of a constipationary nature."

"I know," she sighed to Vinegar. "No need to diagram it all out, or put it to poetry."

"The boys and me . . . well, we was kind of wondering, amongst ourselfs, if'n we might pervert upon your good nature to let us maybe borrow a bottle of that there Let Loose mineral spirit."

Our housekeeper raised an eyebrow. "Vinegar, I believe I'm commencing to understand your particular request." Shaking her head, she opened a cabinet door. "Mineral oil?"

"Yes'm . . . if you please."

She handed him a nearly full bottle of the colorless liquid medication, known among the illiterate afflicted as Let Loose.

"Thanks," said Vinegar. "You expect it right back?"

"No. Please keep it a day or so. But do warn the boys who are . . . knotted up . . . that *it is medicine*, a potent and fast-working laxative." Mrs. Krickitt held up a pair of fingers. "Two tablespoons per dose, and only once a day. Pan Tin will measure it for you."

He left.

So did the three of us, by a roundabout route.

Micah and I, escorting Mrs. Krickitt between us, pretended to be airing an evening stroll; we did so in the general direction where our curiosity itched. Something was up. Because, in the vicinity of the bunkhouse, several assorted scenes of activity were unfolding. Mischief was there, invisible, like carbon monoxide.

Spout was loading two blood-red shells into a double-barrel shotgun. Spider, with a sly face, held a shovel. Domino was busy attaching a small bayonet to the lean end of a long bamboo fishing pole. Pointing to its sharp tip, he grinned.

"Needle," he whispered to Vinegar. "Go hide. But come running soon's you harken our signal."

47

Vinegar, still supervising his precious bottle of new acquired remedy, shuffled over to where Hoofrot was holding a mysterious shoe box.

Vin peeked inside and flinched.

Several men were whispering, motioning, slinking here and yonder on tiptoe. Some, having pulled off their boots, were displaying stockings that had, a decade ago, been white. I wondered what prank they intended to play. Then I saw where all of them seemed to concentrate. Under a tree, a target by the name of Jilly had removed only one boot and one stocking that he held in his hand, and was sleeping soundly. The sound was snoring.

"Ready?" Domino hissed.

"Now!" Hoofrot nodded, after emptying a box of scorpions (which we later learned were all dead) in a half circle around the sleeping newcomer.

Just as Domino jabbed Jilly's naked foot with the fishpole needle, Spout pulled on both scattergun triggers.

WHAM . . . BANG.

The shotgun blasted up a storm of dust around each of Jilly's hips. In ran Spider to pound the ground with his shovel, as if swatting the invaders.

CLANG . . . WOMP . . . CLANK.

"Scorpions!" several pokes hollered at full voice.

Jumping up, Jilly grabbed his needle-pricked foot and began to scream. "I got bit! Oh, good merciful, I be bitten. One them deadly devils just bited me." He stomped a dead scorpion with his boot.

"Can we save this poor sinner's life?" Spout wailed.

Spider shook his head and made a sorrowful face. "No use. Because once a scorpy stings ya, you're nothing but a hard-luck goner. Ain't it tragic?"

"Yup," agreed Hoofrot. "It's curtains."

"Wrong," cackled Vinegar, pretending to gallop from the bunkhouse. "There's hope. This'll save the misfortunate soul."

"Am I gonna die?" Jilly screeched.

"Nope," said Vinegar, "not if you drink this. It could spare your useless life. But you gotta swaller it down quick."

Jilly, not bothering to ask what medicinal miracle was in the bottle, lifted the Let Loose to his desperate lips and tipped up, gulping until the flask was empty.

"Run," Hoofrot told him. "It's your one chance to neutralizationize the poison. Run and jump. High as you can. And pray!"

It was a sight to behold.

Around and around the tree ran a petrified Jilly, jumping up and down, waving his arms, shouting what sounded closer to profanity than prayer. At least he mentioned God. In circles he ran and leaped, begging the Glory Forever to spare his life, until he could final run no more. Wet with sweat, he fell pathetic and panting to the ground.

As his face kissed the dust, we all crowded in for a more intimate squint.

Mr. Ornell Hopple, who usual kept himself aloof from pranksterism, came too. Kneeling, our foreman rested a friendly hand on the patient.

"Whoa it easy, mister," Ornell said. He patted the fallen man's shoulder. "You're fixing to live," he said. "Jilly, maybe to your surprise, I'm keeping you on here. Dom reports that you're a able puncher. No need to doubt what my men tell me. Got it straight?"

Our newest hand nodded.

"You see," Mr. Hop continued, "we got us a zoo of folks on Spur Box, you included. Try'n remember that it ain't a fault or a weakness to git born a yeller Chinaman. Or be a black like Domino, whose face is sporting a few white spots where the pigment quit performing. Vinegar and me, we're olden, and Hoofrot's gimpy lame."

"I understand, boss."

"If you gotta look down on somebody, there's a ample supply of sorrowfuls in The Bent Ace. Some are lazy. Others cheat around a card table. Or pool table. They got stinkers who abuse their horses, their women, and even their kids. Now that's low. Below what I scrape off my boot."

Jilly staggered to his feet. "Mr. Hop, soon's I'm able, I'll square myself with both Tin Pan and Domino. That's a promise."

"Good man." Ornell winked at him. "If you're fixing to call Spur Box a home, treat her homely."

CHAPTER SIX

Father came home.

When I heard the distinctive nicker of a brawny buckskin horse, Highlander, I was in the kitchen, having my stitches yanked out by our all-purpose housekeeper.

Mrs. Krickitt snorted at me.

"Himself," she allowed.

I sat in a kitchen chair, shirt off, my spine becoming an instant crick of sweat. She tried to blot me with a tea towel. But I wouldn't remain dry.

He was out by the barn, barking for Shorty to come and tend to Highlander, rub him down, walk him, and only then turn him out into a night meadow.

Father rarely used the kitchen door. We could hear his boots on the stout planks of our front veranda, the screen door open and close. I didn't hold my breath on purpose. It just always happened, dreading that son and sire would meet, forcing my lungs to exhale.

Heavy feet stopped in the front hallway, while he flipped through a small stack of mail. One letter prompted a growl. Then, footsteps louder and louder, bullying the hardwood floorboards, through the parlor and our unused dining room until . . . there he stood.

Rob Roy MacRobertson.

Although I stared up at the giant man and his white mustache, he didn't bother to return my attention. It was as though I'd faded to invisible. While studying his mail, he spoke only to Mrs. Krickitt. "I'll want coffee in my office."

"In a minute or two," she replied without emotion. "Right now, if you'll notice, I'm extracting thread from your younger son's tore-up carcass."

Father surprised me.

"What happened?" he asked her.

"Tell him." Mrs. Krickitt nudged me. "These just happen to be all *your* stitches, Titus. Not a lace of them's mine."

On my shoulder, once again, I felt a friendly finger tap me; not a spur, but a very subtle prod. Sharp as a whip crack, I almost heard Cowboy Ghost advising me to handle my own explaining. So I did.

"The bunkhouse boys initiated me," I told my father. "In the corral. Had to rope a raw broomtail." My voice steadied. "So I shook out a loop and circled him on the first toss." Forcing a grin, I added, "But he made me eat dirt . . . until I tired him down."

"How old are you now, Titus?"

His question was a shocker. "Sixteen."

"I'd roped my first stringer at coming up fourteen. And afterward, I didn't need no nursemaid to stitch me together." He sighed. "Back in those days, the mustangs kicked a lick more gristly than today." Father's eyes brightened. "Huh. That's what my daddy told *me*. Must be fatherly tradition, bragging how rough life used to be." He winked at me. "Someday you might be puffing the same prattle on *your* son."

"Micah said I hung proud."

"Did he? Well, your brother ought to know. Someday, he'll manage this entire spread. I hope you'll assist him. If you aren't ever stout enough, don't fret about it. Being a cattleman's in Micah's blood. Built like a bull. Like me."

In my mouth, my teeth fought an imaginary bit.

"Who knows?" I told him. "Someday, I could thicken out."

"You?" He grunted his disbelief. "You're sparrow legged, boy. Micah's more my natural son. You were of Eudora's loins and legacy." His throat rumbled. "She dreaded I'd be claiming Micah, so, to confound me for it, she spawned a autumn bloom."

"Enough." It was Mrs. Krickitt who had spoken a single word. "Speak no further, sir, of Eudora. Sully her name and I'll desert you, Mr. Mac." Her voice retreated from its charge. "Remember her with honor, if you please, not for what she took from you, but by treasures endowed."

Father's face darkened.

"Dare you speak to me thus?" he asked her.

"I dare. It's honest MacRobertson truth that I serve Spur Box as housekeeper. Aye, also as your conscience. To prevent your eventual meeting the Almighty without one."

He frowned. "I could banish you."

She held her gray head higher. "Could you? Before you drum me off Spur Box, consider the *parcel*, the land I own here, in my name. Free and clear. Eudora, bless her, saw to that. In town, to Dry Bone, the bankers call my holding a *fee simple absolute*. And I'll dispose of the north parcel *as* I please, and *when* I please."

My father's eyes slowly narrowed. Yet he appeared

hesitant to refute her legal claim to thousands of acres.

"Only," she said, "on my demise will the parcel reunite into the master spread. And," she said confidently, "not until your heirs, Micah or Titus or both, inherit the complete control of Spur Box."

Her defiance was awesome. Heroic. And I was secretly withholding a feverish urge to jump up and cheer.

Their exchange was a Mexican standoff.

Neither one winning.

Each of these seniors was too intelligent to destroy the other. Ironically, they were a team. In a sense, closer than Emma Krickitt had ever been to her departed husband; more intimate, in a business sense, than Rob Roy and Eudora. Fate had married them, in resentment instead of love, yet blessed by a respectful hostility. They alloyed sodium to chlorine, combining to salt the wounds they inflicted upon one another.

They fussed, but they fused.

"Coffee," my father boomed. "Right sudden."

Mrs. Krickitt nodded a casual compliance, as though telling him the coffee would come, not at his speed, but at her convenience.

Before leaving the kitchen, Father glared at our housekeeper one more time. Somehow, I suspected he enjoyed a certain pleasure in their temperamental chess game. "You do possess," he said, "a plenty of swamp-water spunk, Miz Emma." He gave her a slight bow. "I'll credit you that. In full measure."

"Not much," she told him. "But enough to defy *you* whenever you're deserving a dose of my differing."

He laughed and left.

She continued to snake thread out of my flesh. Some of the white was blood-stained brown. When the final stitch got yanked, our housekeeper lowered her kitchen kerosene lamp. "Tee, I'm a wore-out boot. Favor me by taking this coffee to Mr. Mac."

"Go," I said. "Go to bed."

She went. A few seconds passed, and then I heard her Red Cross shoes clumping up the stairs. A white mug of coffee in hand, I went directly through our parlor, and beyond, to my father's office. As I appeared at his door, he looked up.

"Well, this is a surprise service."

"Am I welcome, sir?"

His face softened. "Of course. Come in and stuff a seat. This mail can wait." He must have heard me groan as I sat in one of the black-and-white cowhide visitors' chairs. "Needed some of Emma's sewing to reassemble you?"

"A few stitches."

"You look pretty healthy to me. Guess you proved tougher than a unbroke broomtail."

"It was a draw. Micah claims that I bested the animal, and he wouldn't fib. But don't ask me to judge the outcome, on account my eyes were shut tight. I just hung to the rope, and dragged, until the mustang tired."

"Think you'll make a hand after all?"

"Hope so, once I finish high school."

"This is summer, boy. Now's the time to ranch it full-time. Not just assisting Micah at the smithy. When I was your age . . ." He stopped. "How to bore your children. Keep bringing up yesterday's heroes in the first person."

"Father, it isn't boring. I enjoy hearing about old days, and how Mr. Max, and later on Mr. Mac, you, obtained this ranch and started running cows. Back when Mother was—"

The abrupt chilling of his face cut me short, and I knew I'd wounded someone I cared not to hurt.

"Another time, Titus. Off you go. I'll confer with Ornell Hopple, to find you a task to tackle. Good night."

"Good night, sir."

"One more thing, boy. Growing up involves many a stretch of stitches, and more'n one bruise. In humans as well as in animals, a whelp matures only when it must. Not until."

Falling asleep, I dreamed of my old Cowboy Ghost. We were again in the barn together, yet all I heard was a symphony of the night: a choir of crickets, roosting swallows in the gray rafters, a single *cluck* of a hermit hen. Plus a waft of wind that attempted to squeeze between a pair of planks, couldn't, and roared annoyance.

Sort of like Rob Roy.

CHAPTER SEVEN

✕☐

Tee," my brother told me, "you got a natural knack with horses. You handle 'em right well."

Pleased by Micah's comment, I bent, nested, and viced the mare's hoof solidly between my skinny knees. Micah had taught me: Always heft up a left front leg first, as it's the closest to where a rider climbs aboard, and thus puts the animal at ease.

My brother was wearing only boots, faded blue denim pants, and a stout leather apron the color of molasses. His hogshead chest was hairy and sweaty wet. A massive arm and hand held a smith's hammer.

"Now," he said, "cut the hoof exact as I showed you. Perfect. Feel how soft and pulpy the paring is? Sign of a sound animal. I don't trust a hard-hoofed horse."

He pounded a hot shoe on the anvil table with a mighty and metallic *clang*. Dunking the shoe into his cooling tub, Micah waited for the steamy hiss to melt away. "All right, now we fit iron to her crescent. Good. Just enough frog to absorb shock."

As taught, I pounded six nails down through the shoe and into the mare's hoof until they bristled out below. My tongs twisted off their points flush with the horny hoof barrel. After filing, I could see the countersunk nails. Six little stars of silver.

Then, with a fullering bar, I managed to rim the shoe all around to make it marry the hoof.

"Good work," I heard a familiar voice say. Looking up from the hoof between my knees, I saw Ornell Hopple.

"Thanks," I said.

"Tee, do the ranch a favor," the foreman said. "Saddle your sorrel and canvass the south quarter. Nowheres else, boy. On account if you ain't returned here at least two hours before dark, we'll know whichaway your trouble lies."

"Will do, Mr. Hop."

"Round as many strays as you can comfortable herd in a bunch. Head 'em north. Know where be and where going. Soon's the sun is three quarter across day, point your animal toward the ranch. Cows or no cows. Hear?"

Bending him an obedient grin, I saluted.

While I was in the kitchen, hurriedly stuffing myself

and a noon pouch with biscuits, Mrs. Krickitt added a few extra precautions.

"When you come to a lengthy stand of burnt pines, barren as witch brooms, turn your horse and travel north again. Beyond the char's nothing except a swamp. Snakes, gators, and those brown recluse spiders. All three can finish you in a nibble."

Biting a cookie, I nodded.

"What did Mr. Hop tell you?" she asked.

"Same as you. The ramrod wants to know *where* I'm going, and *when* I'll be back."

As she stood at the sink, her back to me, she scrubbed egg from a fry pan. Her sleeves were rolled up, displaying the white wrinkled knobs of her elbows.

"Long time ago, my husband rode off to scare up cows," she said. "Didn't bother to ride where he'd intended. Horse come home after dark under a empty saddle, and 'twas close to a week before the searchers located his body, what little weren't eaten by a army of critters. Large and small."

She sighed.

"Do as Mr. Hopple directs," she told me. "Taking prudent care is not a sign of cowardly. It's solid sense. Because the wilder the territory, the wiser a lone rider has to be."

"Yes'm."

Just as I banged the kitchen's screen door, she yelled after me, "For supper, I might be baking a carrot cake, with cinnamon and raisins. If you're late gathering your person to home, Micah gets *your* share."

I smiled.

She'd given me both stick and carrot.

Riding south at a brisk trot, it didn't take me long to lose sight of our house and barns. Being alone made me respect the stretchy span of Spur Box. She was a load of land. "Florida," our cowhands often remarked, "is long country."

South of Spur Box lay nothing except thousands of square miles of unpopulated and uncultivated desolation, endless swamps and sloughs. Silent black water beneath the mossy gray garlands cascaded from countless bell-bottomed cypress trees.

My horse and I passed cows, almost all with a ✕☐ brand on the flank. Loners, strayed from the main herd, wandered to become hermits on hoof. Made no sense collecting them while heading south. In two hours, I'd wheel my mount, swap ends, and start north. Then we'd round the rovers.

"Today," I told Ginger as she loped along easy, "we're going to perform everything right and follow Mr. Hop's order to the letter. No variation. We'll show 'em. Before dark, we might come whooping home behind every orphan we can locate, wet or dry."

Licking my lips, I already tasted carrot cake.

Pulling my animal to a halt, I climbed down under shade to rest her and me. "Easy, Tee," I said aloud. "Best you fight that itch to impress your family. Today's not a prove-it-or-else."

Later, in control of my boyish dreams and my horse, as well as the chore itself, I spun Ginger a one-eighty and happily headed due north. We certain collected. Like a fool, I hadn't bothered to leave Spur Box with a rope looped on my horn. So, using my hat as a quirt, I managed to lean out of the saddle enough to swat the hinders of stragglers by hat and by holler.

"H'ya. H'ya. Heeyahhh!"

We got lucky. Behind palmetto, there she stood. A mature cow. Maybe lost. Perhaps with a yen to rejoin a bunch and sleep among other cows. A few solitary sundowns had possible convinced her that our ranch was home. Not here. A whack of my hat persuaded her into a cow's version of haste. The younger and smaller cows seemed to have a hanker to follow her. As though she'd wore a clanking neck bell.

Somehow, we returned.

A score of cows plodded to Spur Box. Only a few head behind. Trouble is, I couldn't just leave it alone. No, I had to hotdog it; approaching our ranch proper, I felt compelled to spook all my newfounders into a sprint.

"Yahoo!"

Sun was west. A few punchers had already assembled in the bunkhouse to wash for another of Tin Pan's mountainous meals. Except for Micah and Ornell.

There they stood. Looking south. No doubt a mite alarmed because I returned late.

Here I came, whacking a hat to my horse, behind two dozen Spur Box steers. We all should've eased up. But no, the beardless boy had to thunder into view, through dust, all hoofs beyond control. Perhaps they were too happy to get home. Or, like me, too doggone brainless. A few of the anxious piled into the fence, then through it, and wood splintered in assorted directions. All I saw was hurry-up animals and Ornell shaking his head as though he wondered how come a sane couple such as Rob Roy and Eudora could've bred a lunatic.

At full gallop, I kicked out of the saddle.

But not very graceful.

As my boot skidded into unsure footing, there was no way to recover, so I sort of met a fence. Along with a confused cow. She crowded me something fearful, busted a section of the chicken yard, and then scampered off to the north. Through Tin's flowers.

Nobody spoke to me. Not even Mrs. Krickitt, when

I final unsaddled, rubbed Ginger dry, made it to the kitchen, and soaped.

The carrot cake near to choked me.

It certain was no cinch falling asleep that night, not when I was feeling like such a fool. Lying there in the dark, for a moment I imagined the voice of my Cowboy Ghost: mature, steady, seasoned by decades of chores, cattle, and raw ranching. His voice sounded cold, gray, rougher than wet weather.

"Time," he said. "Give yourself time. No need to stretch up to manhood in a single day."

CHAPTER EIGHT

Three down," Mrs. Krickitt said.

Coming up from the bunkhouse, once inside the kitchen, she soaped her hands at the sink. Then joined my father, Micah, and me at the table.

Father grumbled a gripe.

"Cattle ranching," he commented to nobody in particular, "is one flapdoodle ailment after another." His hand pounded the faded pink oilcloth. "I'm fixing to visit down yonder and boot both sides of Tin Pan's butt."

"Go slow," Mrs. Krickitt warned Father. Making him wait, she poured herself a mug of coffee. "Because it isn't Tin's blame."

"Why ain't it?"

Our housekeeper took a sip. "Seems the three waddies took their rightfully deserved day off to visit Dry Bone, shoot pool, lose at blackjack, and swallow The

Bent Ace dry. That they handled. But nary the hot-gut cookery of Mex Town. Our unlucky three made it home toting food poisoning and then cranked up a puking contest."

"Which three?"

"Shorty, Fat Cat, and the new fellow, Jilly."

"What did Ornell say?"

"Well," she said, "he's inherited a trio of fevers hotter than the Devil's drawers. They might recover in a couple of days. Trouble is, they'll be weakly for several more. Three men light for the drive. He claims, in a pinch, he'll make do with a extra pair."

Something happened in the next second that shocked me.

"Tee 'n' I can go. That is, if it pleases Hop to take us along," Micah said, and then made a slight face at Father. "You know how he balks mixing hands and family."

"Ornell needs *three* men. You're *one*. I'd go, but one heart attack is plenty. I mightn't last. You best canter to Dry Bone, direct to The Bent Ace, and rope some out-of-work drover. Tell the hunk of scum it pays a dollar a day, and found."

"Mr. Hop hires on more'n scum," Micah said. "For a sidekick, I'd select my brother over any saddle tramp." He grinned my way.

Father, to my amazement, said, "So would I, Micah. But he's still sixteen." In frustration, Mr. Mac's hand curled up the curving tips of his white mustache.

"Time was," Micah said softly, "when every cow-hand was merely a kid. Being young's no proof of unworthy."

It sure was a jolt when Father suddenly rested a paternal paw on my shoulder. "You're right, Micah. This lad has got to hew the hardwood sometime, so maybe it ought to start today."

Mrs. Krickitt had held her tongue for over a minute, breaking her own indoor record. "Were I the ramrod of Spur Box, or any outfit, I'd take whoever's got the gumption to go. Micah's gone a number times. It's Tee's turn to deserve his keep. What's more, Micah reports that Tee is able around horses."

"You ain't the foreman, lady," Father muttered.

"No. Neither are you. Ornell Hopple stays because you promised he'd hold a free hand to the ribbons. He reins it able to profit. So check Ornell. If he approves . . . Titus goes."

"Miss Emma, I hate it whenever you talk sense." Father stood. "Micah, best consult Hop. Tell him we cornered two men. Tee, come to my office. There's matters to discuss. It's time for a chick's gizzard to peck up gravel and grind corn."

He left and I followed.

"Sit," he ordered me, indicating one of the two black-and-white Holstein-cowhide chairs.

I sat. So did himself, flanked on either side by a few of his tarnishing boxing trophies. High on the wall, facing me, hung the long-horned skull of a giant steer, a white arid souvenir of life now deceased. It was pallid bone: sightless eyes, twin craters of a voided blackness. Horns no longer able to hook. Teeth beyond grazing. Perhaps it was Father's reminder of years ago, and how proud he once stood.

"Titus, a moment back it hit me square that as I been growing older, you've growed up." His sun-baked face studied me, the lines deepening and Scottish blue eyes boring like swords. "What's your age? Sorry I keep forgetting."

"I'm . . . I'm sixteen now."

His eyes softened to a gentler blue, as though viewing a cherished place far away. Or perhaps a person.

"Sixteen." A big hand cupped his knee with a thud. "Ironic. That's how long you been living and I been close to dead."

"I understand, sir. Honest."

As though trying to deny all emotion, Father shifted his ponderous weight, causing the chair to creak a few times. "I'm not dead, but dying. Perhaps of self-pity. If a man affords pitying to another person, it's a virtue, although to *respect* someone else is far nobler. But when he pities hisself, it's flabby."

Leaning back a bit, Father lifted his left leg to rest a boot on his right knee.

"You haven't talked to me like this before," I told him.

"Enough of sentiment," he said, in a voice becoming icy. A thick finger began to spin the rowel wheel on the spur of his horizontal boot. Instead of looking direct at me, his gaze shifted to the oval-framed photograph of Mother that hung on the wall beside the window. "Feelings," he almost growled, "don't amount to rat squat. What counts is action, what a man *does* as opposed to what he feels."

Hauling in a deep breath, I bit the bullet. "Please, talk to me about my mother. What little I know is nothing more than stories, from Micah and by Mrs. Krickitt. But neither one knew her as you did. And I want to."

"No!" he boomed.

"You ought. Because I am *her* son as well as yours, and I got a honest right to learn about my mother. Okay, so it pains you to recall what happened."

"Aye, it do."

"Then spill a bit of the burden on me. Grief is a family chore, and I can shoulder my share."

"Do understand, Titus. Now just isn't the time. Instead, let's look ahead for the benefit of our ranch."

I nodded, studying an iron replica of the face of our branding iron that sat on his desk. A spur and a box.

Cold steel. Despite its chill, the metal seemed to be white hot, an object I wouldn't care to touch for fear of the strong stink of its burn.

"Pay attention, boy. Look at me when I'm talking. A cattle drive is no Sunday social. Only the drovers, who be hot, dirty, smelly sons of Hell, can abide the easterly trek that you and Micah are so eager to take. Men who do such, Tee, ain't no better and no worse than any other outfit's punchers. It's a dung job for dust eaters. A rancher don't hire on a genius to do cowhanding. Mostly they're a mess of simple men able to breathe trail grit, swallow cold beans, and sleep on cactus under nothing except a tore-up blanket and rain."

His description excited me.

"Well, I want to be one of them."

Father shook his head. "That's odd. Not even Micah aspires to that lowly station." He paused. "Your bro, however, has always been one of the boys. A rock, your big brother."

"But," I said, "Micah's not another Rob Roy MacRobertson, even though you wish it and are convinced it's true. There's a chance, sir, you might be mistaken."

My own brassy tone was biting me by its defiance. Not impolite. Mere a rare rush of daring.

"Tee, you're becoming one uppity pup." He stared at me. "Micah doesn't dare spout off so cussed lippy. You got more bowel than my big boxer."

"I apologize, Father."

"Dang ought." He almost grinned. "Golly be, I take to somebody who's got a lick of salt. Backbone. Grit. Whatever *sass* be called, you're chewing a pinch of it in your cheek."

"As you suggested, look ahead. Tell me more about a cattle drive. What exact is Mr. Hop going to expect from me?"

"Years back, I got broke in when Spur Box was a real ripsnort of a beef outfit. Who bossed it? My pap: Maxwelton Ramsay MacRobertson." He took a breath, spun the wheel on his boot, then continued. "Boy, anytime you verdict *me* hard, remember this. I cut teeth on a tyrant."

"I want to prove out."

"Bully. Because it's two hundred slow miles without a roof. On horseback you'll zigzag four hundred. You're fixing to slumber wet. Or ride thirsty. You'll fall out your saddle to naught but a skimpy night. Before dawn, a tired-out waddy will kick you awake to say it's your turn to coddle cows. Five hundred plus of them. You'll inhale their dust and their deviltry. When you're the worst tuckered, a Florida thunder-boomer will strike the sky to ebon. Every cow will panic, stampede, and attempt to trample you into nothing but another sip of sand." His eyes narrowed. "On top of all that, there's more'n one gang of cowdiggers."

"What are those?

"Thieves. Freeloaders that want a share of what we sweated to earn. It's possible you won't meet up; then again . . ." He looked into my eyes. "I'm grateful Micah will be with you." He sighed. "But it's still a ripper of a ride."

"I'll hack it."

"Precious better. If'n ya fail, our drovers will demean you to something they'd wipe off a butt. You best pull equal." Father leaned closer to me. "There won't be a Emma Krickitt to unsnot your nose."

He stood.

So did I.

Once again, as we were standing close, I became aware of my father's height, weight, and overall stature. Gray but granite hard.

"Now I know about a drive," I told my Father. "But I'm not fixing to quit. It's only a chore."

Rob Roy MacRobertson stared down at me, as though wondering if his second son, the one he thought of as Eudora's child, possessed the gumption to measure up.

"Titus," he said, "for you, this cattle drive'll be a fork in the trail. Your guts." He pointed at my crotch. "Or your gelding."

CHAPTER NINE

I crept to bed early.

Even so, I certain wasn't geared up for Micah's shaking my shoulder at four o'clock the following morning.

"Titus, it's time. Tee, wake up now. Git dressed and go assist Tin Pan, as Mr. Hop expects."

"It's . . . the middle of night."

"Maybe so. But you don't want Ornell again to look sorry at you, then chase you back under Mrs. Krickitt's apron. Do you?"

"No." I thought for a second. "Don't guess I do."

"Then hustle your carcass."

Five minutes later, I reported to Tin Pan, who was already chattering like it was nearing noon. He put me loading foodstuffs into his chucky, or cook wagon. Sacks of potatoes; bags of carrots, onions, beans, and rice; white slabs of salt pork. Flour, sugar, eggs, baking powder, a tub of lard, pork bellies for bacon. Bars of bitter chocolate. A couple barrels of oranges. Tins of coffee and tea.

"No beef?" I asked Tin.

The question prompted a toothy laugh. "Ha! Beef walk."

His answer made me feel fooly before we'd as much as budged a inch off home.

A tool and tack wagon was also being packed, by Dom and Vinegar, under the hawk's eye of our foreman. Little escaped Mr. Hop's notice. Without ceremony, Ornell tossed out a spade that had a cracked handle. A dull double-bit axe made a similar exit.

"Domino"—the boss spoke privately to him—"even in daylight, ol' Vinegar can't see enough to piss a straight stream, say nothing of darksome. Check it yourself. Hear?"

Dom nodded. "I gotcha, Mr. Hop."

"Inspect every foot of rein, harness; work all the buckles prior to loading. Bring extra saddle blankets for every man. And a spare saddle. Go over the list with Micah. He'll be driving."

At sunup I was allowed to grub a breakfast with the hands in the bunkhouse mess.

Ordinarily, I'd a been hungrier than happy. But about

five minutes earlier, Tin told me to empty the three puke buckets (the ones partly filled by Shorty, Fat Cat, and Jilly). Then I hosed them clean. None of the three thanked me. No need. They were flat on their backs, moaning, and still feverish.

So, at dawn, it dang *dawned* on me that I wasn't about to become a cowhand. My title would be Junior Assistant Tin Pan.

"Mr. Hopple," I made the mistake of asking our top hand (who, I'd somehow forgotten, was busy sorting out a hundred importants), "am I to hack at this miserable job every day of the cattle drive? Is this all I get to do?"

Unpleased, he squared at me.

"Tee, right now, and until we stagger home again, you'll perform whatever duty you're told. One puppy-dog whimper, and you'll be ordered to retreat so fast your nose'll bleed." He placed both fists to his hipbones. "Clear?"

"Clear. Gotcha, Mr. Hop," I said, trying to echo Domino.

Breakfast in our bunkhouse mess didn't look a lot like a meal. Instead, it was a mayhem. Cowhands were whacking at their plates as if Tin's flapjacks were fixing to run loose and had to be trapped, shot, or skinned alive. Had the grits and scrambles got dumped into a pig trough, nary a Spur Boxer would have noticed or cared.

Nor did a mouthful of Tin's fluffy biscuits muffle gab.

Crumbs spouted to punctuate every oath.

What was the word we'd learned in school, in biology class? *Omnivores*: critters who'd eat everything and anything. So here sat I at the bunkhouse mess, surrounded by omnivores in stained hats and scuffed boots. Tin Pan's job, I realized, wasn't to prepare dining for human consumption. He merely slopped the hogs.

I loved it!

Mrs. Krickitt, needless to say, was not present to order me to chew before swallowing, remove elbows off a table, or sit up straight.

Unlike her, nobody in a bunkhouse mess uses the word *proper*.

There I sat in Paradise, between Vinegar, who didn't wash, and Spider, who, as far as I could observe, seldom bothered to cut anything into smaller pieces. He merely stuffed a undivided pancake into his gaping maw. Whatever he couldn't fork whole, Spider gulped down his gullet by using his free hand.

Coffee slopped all over everywhere and everyone. Brown drops of it beaded into the sugar bowl by way of uncaring spoons.

Milk created a chain of little white puddles. No one noticed. As I sat there, in rapture, I was amazed that Mr. Hop didn't provide armed guards to prevent our cowhands from devouring each other. Food that hadn't been drooled onto the long table had found a home on the floor. No matter. Eager fingers scooped it up and returned it to either one plate or another.

It was a belle of a brawl.

And there, above it all, stood the smiling and reigning conductor: Tin Pan. For some weird reason perhaps known only to our cook, Tin actual gloated in watching (and also hearing) people eat.

Into the stream I tumbled, swept by a current of animal appetites: Tin's chow, as everyone on Spur Box (even Mrs. Krickitt) claimed, was good wholesome grub. Quality and quantity. Around me the consumption of cookery became contagious. The more I listened to them eat, the more ravenous I became.

Across from me, Micah also spaded in.

This was certain not Micah's first meal among our hands. Now, at a age of twenty-nine, he had already earned respect from the crew at Spur Box. No, not because they'd known he'd be the next Rob Roy, but because my brother was, to them, sort of a somebody. A celebrity! He was Mr. Micah Samson MacRobertson, a boxer, someone able to floor almost any other man with only one punch. Iron Micah.

As I sat there, gnawing a warm biscuit, I got tempted to ponder if any of our Spur Box cowpokes were aware that I'd eventual be Mr. Titus Timothy MacRobertson.

My guess?

Nary a one.

Yet, to me, it didn't rightful matter. Because I was resolved that, before long, all of them (including Micah and Mr. Rob Roy) would know me. This cattle drive could contribute to my cause. No way could I wilt or wither. Regardless of pain, fear, or fatigue, little ol' Tee would have to muster his muscle (what little there was of it) in order to prove out.

A question tapped my shoulder.

Prove to whom?

CHAPTER TEN

✶▢

We moved out.

Tin Pan and I rode the grub wagon.

A cattle drive (one that's efforting to contain half a thousand white-faced red cattle, a unruly band of about two score broncs, wagons, and punchers) doesn't progress beyond a tortoise speed.

Took a day to vacate Spur Box.

First off, cows ain't exactly eagerish to depart. For them, the party is right here at home, on good grass, limestone and calcium rich, that profits the bones of all four-footed grazers. It ain't somewheres else. To a cow, walking isn't worth the effort. It's just something to do while you chew.

Years ago, I got given my own horse.

A sorrel mare with a golden mane and tail. I'd named her Ginger, as she favored a few flecks of seasoning that

Mrs. Krickitt freckled upon her apple dumplings. Ginger was the only horse to feel comfortable between my legs. I'd natural presumed that she'd belong on the drive.

Wrong.

"No," Ornell had earlier told me.

"Why not?"

He sighed. "Because, if she gits turned loose, as she'll have to be, amongst them other bangtailers, many of which are half broke or half gator, the wilders may kill her. And if you hobble her, they'll close in and chomp her to bits. Once she's fallen over, they will stomp that pretty sorrel to beyond dead." He paused. "You want that?"

"No." Yet a question was scraping at my insides. "Why would the other horses do such?"

"Jealousy. Simple that. Titus, don't ask me a how-come—they sense it. They actual do. Sooner or later, animals will let loose a human trait, as men sometimes behave like a beast. Don't ponder it right or wrong. Just occurs. So start observing *what's so*. And tolerate."

"How'll I do for a mount?"

Ornell spat.

"Titus, anytime you git assigned a herding duty, be it during the dark before first light, or late in the day when you're so wrung out you'd scream to lie down, you'll have to shake a loop in order to rope yourself a strange. You can do it. I saw ya."

What Ornell was saying was causing my staring at him. In disbelief. But then I remembered mornings on Spur Box. Every hand had to coil and toss over the unwilling head of a raw, a stringer that cottoned to kick, or bite, or drag a puncher about a mile closer to Georgia.

"I'll do it, Mr. Hopple."

"Perform it with no griping. The other waddies working with you will be beat to bone. Tired through. You're to relieve hands that are liken to a old stocking. Wore out and stinky. Regardless of how you're feeling, they register a passel worse."

"Okay," I said. "I'll cut it."

Mr. Hop slowly nodded. "A drive be a business undertaking, Titus. It's hardly a trip into Dry Bone to attend school. You gotta pull."

"What do I do?"

"Focus. Concentrate all your gumption on a *here-now*. Mere the chore at hand. That's what manhood is, Titus. It's a tending of today."

Ornell rode off.

Bumping along in a chucky, with Tin Pan mumbling at the mules, didn't enthuse me much. However, I suffered through morning and part of a endless afternoon. There was no noon meal except oats for the horses. The cowhands changed mounts, pulling their saddles off the sweat-darkened backs of their morning stringers in order to slap leather on a fresh. For hands, there wasn't a breath of rest.

We'd brung only four mules.

Two remained hitched to Micah's tack wagon and two to ours. With rarely a pause, our mules leaned into their collars, hauling slow and steady without a complaining honk. Tin had named them: Right and Wong. It took me a while to figure just why Tin Pan had chosen the two names. Some hand would point at either mule, then ask, "Is this'n Right?"

That's when Tin pulled his only punch line. "Wong," he'd say, and about fall down laughing.

Tin was a one-joke comic.

Spout appeared on a foamy, tired-looking horse. His rope stretched straight back for twenty feet to the neck of another stringer fighting the loop. Twisting, jaws open.

"Tee," said Spout, "Mr. Hop ordered me to present ya with a animal. She's all yourn. So strap a seat to her and then go assist Bagpipe, who's riding drag." He passed me the loose end of the rope. "You got a bandanna?"

"No," I said, feeling a empty back pocket.

"Here," he said. "Better use mine. I got a extra. Unless you're fixing to inhale half of Florida and cough consumptionary." He handed me his bandanna, in which there was already more cow dust than there was on the ground.

"Thanks."

"You need help to tack?"

"Naw," I said, like three varieties of tomfool, reasoning that a horse is a horse, and knowing how simple it usual was to saddle Ginger. "No thanks."

This horse didn't have a name. Range horses don't. Yet she certain had herself a disposition. Knotting the loose end of the rope to a hinge eye on the tailgate of Tin's wagon, I jumped down and trotted to where Micah was driving the other team of mules. Fetching my saddle and bridle, I returned.

The merriment began.

Tin Pan halted his mules, maybe wondering what miracle I'd planned to do next, and shouted helpful instructions in Chinese.

That hellion of a horse, the one that Spout had selected for me, flattened back her ears, rolled her eyes white, and kicked Florida topsoil in near to ten directions. As I approached her left flank, a sudden toss of her brainless head knocked me flat, saddle and all. Tin continued his foreign-language lecture, pointing first at me, then the horse. No doubt Tin considered himself older and wiser than I by far and an expert on horse handling.

Never had I seen Tin Pan mounted. Give him this: Except for the mules, Tin was smart enough to avoid critters of any size or nature, from a bull to Cleopatra.

This lack of experience, however, failed to prevent his shouting and gesturing. Yet he final proved useful by scampering to the tack wagon and bringing back my brother.

"Tee," Micah asked, "you into trouble?"

I nodded. "A speck."

"This barbarian Spout brung you as a prank. She's near unrid. Once a moon, maybe, if all the other beasts are either dead or dying. I seen her buck Spider so high in the air that he near starved to death before he landed."

It hit me. This cusser had tossed off *Spider*? No way! Spider, lean and lanky, could straddle and then outlast any crossbreed that our Almighty had ever created. This included a bear, gators, and at least half of the upstairs livestock at The Bent Ace. Few, he boasted, had bucked him off.

"What'll I do?"

"Watch."

Without another word, Micah followed the taut rope to the mare's head, yanked a brutal yank, encircled the mare's neck with his beefy blacksmith arms, and choked her quiet.

"Saddle her, Tee."

I did so, and quick. As I tried to tighten the cinch, her belly inflated like she was settled and expecting an overdue foal. Micah saw it. Using the knee of a stout leg, he thumped the ornery animal's underside. She expelled enough gas, out of both her ends, to fill a blimp. As Micah maintained his choke hold, I cinched and bridled her.

"Want me to climb on?" I asked.

"Not right sudden."

Micah, all two hundred and fifty pounds of him, mounted the mare, put heels to her hide, and rode her really hard for a distance. Wheeling her, he then returned. My mare quit her prancing. She stood stiller than stone, puffing like a locomotive.

"Your turn," Micah said, dismounting.

I forked her, prepared to be the receiving end of a dose of discomfort. The horse seemed, in her crazy way, to be grateful of half the weight on her spine, and behaved.

"Now," Micah said, slowly coiling Spout's rope, "you ride that reputation everywhere you can, at a gallop. Allow the hands notice. Because she's made several of those waddies eat turf. They'll have trouble believing their eyes. Keep the horse moving. Don't give her no time to think about herself or *you* about *yourself.*"

"I gotta go ride with Bagpipe."

"Do it."

"Thanks a bunch, Micah."

He grinned. "What's a brother for?"

At a rapid dust-kicking canter, I rode by several of the Spur Box boys, wahooing my hat to let 'em know how I enjoyed being one of them. Their eyes popped.

Bagpipe, when I arrived at the rear of our slow-moving cows, stared at me, the horse, and back to me again. He had a bandanna over his face to strain the sand before swallowing it, so I couldn't see his mouth. Yet because he still was talkative ol' Bagpipe, I figured it was open.

In shock.

"Tee," he asked, when he could recover enough to speak, "how come, of all the ponies to pick, you selected that Devil's Daughter?"

Riding circles around him to show off, I happened to think of something smart-alecky to say. So, holding back a good chuckle, I said it.

"Next time, I'll rope one with more spunk."

CHAPTER ELEVEN

✕☐

Bagpipe and I rode drag.

This job, I soon appreciated, is the absolute worst position to work at while pushing beef. The rear end of misery. Ranching's rectum.

In rain, you're riding into a shower of everyone else's splattering mud. Under sunshine, when the earth's dry, two thousand hoofs are filling the atmosphere with grit. Half of it falls to the ground. The rest we inhale. A dragger and his horse plod along in the center of a choking cloud of cow crud.

A cow's a simple machine. She absorbs grass and water, then expels gas, urine, or manure. Multiply this process by five hundred, and you'll predict our fragrant whereabouts.

"Yup," said Bagpipe through his bandanna. "I certain do cherish this job we got. It's a pip."

All I could do was hear him and laugh, because the afternoon happened to be sunny, dry, and dusty. Cloudy, one might say, in jest. Visibility zero.

"Know why I enjoy drag riding so much? Well, I tell ya," Bag said. "It's a real luxury for a cowhand to see what he's breathing."

Another thing I learned.

No cowboy can hurry a cow.

She (or he) moves at her own speed. Slow. Then, by late afternoon, after being prodded, poked, yelled at, and even whacked by a lariat, she quits moving slow. She stops. It's a cow's decision how many miles she'll saunter in a day. I don't reckon how many. Some secret formula.

It's the opposite of a stampede.

When one steer stops, *they all stop*. Five filthy hundred of them, as though a bell cow blowed a whistle, and then bellowed through a bullhorn: "Quitting time, girls."

Horses can, if raked by the rowel of a spur, move out hasty. But while serving a stretch of drag, a cowhand and his horse progress at the exact identical speed of the herd's slowest or laziest cow.

Side by side, breathing in the beauty, Bagpipe and I rode slowly along, almost knee to knee. Staring straight ahead at the often-productive red rumps of Spur Box cattle, each contributing to keep Florida wet or green.

"The wages is meager," Bagpipe said, "but, on the advantage side, you gotta admit, riding drag, we certain can enjoy a view."

Before I could reply, Bagpipe spotted a stray and spurred his gelding to immediate action, cutting back and to his left. Looking where his horse was headed, I saw a large cow. Usual, the brood cows stayed at Spur Box because market steers are smaller, lighter, younger, and butcher at 1000 to 1300 pounds. Rarely are they mature and pregnant.

This cow was both.

In fact, she sudden left the drive in order to keep lonesome, enjoy privacy, and drop a calf. And she did. It was quick and bloody and then all hers. After biting the cord, the cow started licking her newborn, cleaning him, nudging him to stand, nurse, and live.

I rode close to look.

By the time the Devil's Daughter and I arrived, Bagpipe already had circled a loop. As the newborn calf was struggling to stand up to a wobble, the rope noose settled around the little wet critter's neck. Turning his horse, Bag jerked the calf off its feet and yanked it back toward the herd.

"What are you doing?" I yelled at him.

Bagpipe shrugged. "Only way to convince that cow to foller. Hear that calf bawling? Don't fret about it, boy.

The little one'll choke to death in a minute. I know. Because I done this sorry act a hundred awful times. And can't abide it."

"It's cruel."

"Life's tough. This bothering you?"

"Yes," I told him.

Pulling a knife out of his boot, Bagpipe handed it to me. "Here then. Go back there and cut its throat. I'll pull it dead, and that mother'll still foller after the smell." I took the knife's handle. "Well," said Bag, "go do it. Ain't no way we can rescue the calf. But we gotta keep that full-growed cow moving with the bunch. You understand?"

"Sort of."

"Do it fast, Tee. Don't lollygag, or Big Mama'll charge at you, horns foremost. One slash under his jaw will finish him."

"I don't like this," I said.

"Nobody do. Ranching ain't violins."

Bag rode along with me, hefting up the rope enough to raise the calf's head. The bulging brown eyes looked at me as though knowing that life was short and miserable. About to end. Leaning from the saddle, I slashed the young white throat. Blood spurted. All I could do was study the shiny reddened knife in my trembling hand, unable to believe that I'd played a part in such a senseless slaughter.

"Use your shirttail," Bagpipe said, "to wipe the blade clean. We ain't fixing to carry rust."

Bag proved accurate.

The brood cow followed her bleeding calf, now motionless at the end of Bagpipe's lariat. I looked over my shoulder several times. Bag didn't. He just sat a pony, staring straight ahead. To him, what happened was one minor event in a long, hard-working cowpoke of a day.

After the knife blade got shirt wiped (my shirt) and returned to the boot of its owner, Bag unwound his rope's free end from his saddle and then twisted it around the horn of mine.

"Here," he said. "About another minute and that calf's carcass will bleed dry. Big Mama's near already forgot she dropped him. You'll see."

Bagpipe galloped off to haze two other laggard strays. To watch him sit a horse was better than hearing music. Every motion did easy. He and his animal were one graceful entity, as though they'd not been asked to work, but to waltz.

He returned.

"It's sorrowful sad," Bagpipe said, lifting the down corner of his bandanna so's he could spit brown.

"What is?"

"This long country called Florida. Not much open

range left. Be fewer cattle drives. Ranchers'll have to prod steers up a incline ramp, into a truck, in order to market their beefs."

"How do you know this for certain? You hardly ever stray off Spur Box except for Saturday night in Dry Bone."

"Your pa heard it at the Cattleman's gathering. Mr. Mac told Ornell, who told Vinegar, who told Fat Cat, who told Dom . . ."

"Okay," I said, "I'll pass the news to Cleopatra."

With a glance behind, Bag pointed at the mother cow. "See there, Tee? She ain't chasing her young'un no more. Forgot. Cows are stupid. Almost as brainless as the humans who herd 'em on horseback."

With a easy flick of his wrist, Bagpipe snaked his lasso off the dusty dead calf and coiled it, returning it to his saddle. Back of us, the calf's forlorn remains lay on the late-afternoon sand, forgotten, I presumed, by everyone but me.

"A shame," I said, "to waste a calf."

"Nope," said Bagpipe. Shifting the reins to his right hand, he scratched inside his shirt as though chasing chiggers across his chest. "In nature, Tee, nothing gits wasted. Not a fallen tree or a fallen calf." Gesturing with a upward toss of his head, he added, "Look up yonder."

I looked.

A lone buzzard was drawing black circles on a light misty sky. As I watched, a second buzzard flew in from nowhere.

"Them buzzards," Bag told me, "will sudden start to beak the meat off that little dead calf. Then crows. After dark, rats. Tomorrow, the skeleton will be licked clean by grubs and a thousand fire ants. All them gotta eat. Dead animals help green the grass. It won't waste, Tee. Nothing actual do."

"You're some philosopher," I said.

"Me? Like fun. Titus, I certain don't know a whole much, but leastwise, I got it ample figured who I be."

"What are you?"

"Mr. Content." He spat again. "More'n twenty year ago, I found me a decent home, working cows for your daddy's outfit. Hard labor? Boy, cards don't git dealt no leaner. Long hours and low pay. But I stay on, because Mr. Ornell Hopple rams honest and rides a straight fence." He sighed. "I got no education. On a good day, if given a hour to consider, I can lick a pencil to write my front name, which is Bartholomew."

"And you're a happy man."

Bagpipe nodded. "You betcha. Titus, the secret of joyfulness is hawg simple. I'm happy. Because I know who and what I be."

* * *

The cows stopped.

We all took turns attacking Tin Pan's supper. Beans, corn dodgers, boiled onions and rice and peppers. Fried beef. Then a orange for everybody. Even me. Never knew a single orange could swallow so sweet. Living in Florida, I'd eaten myself ample. But here, in the darksome of a sundown, among all the other punchers, one solitary orange tasted Gospel good.

In a daze, requiring no sleeping pill, all I recollect is unscrolling a damp, gritty, and smelly blanket underneath and between the wheels of Tin Pan's chucky, pulling off my boots, keeling over, and passing out.

If that old Cowboy Ghost had somehow ridden and sweated alongside of me this day, he'd a been equal done in.

CHAPTER TWELVE

It four o'clock."

Wrong. Something ran amuck in my dream about a special girl that I'd begun to like a lot.

"Please, Mr. Titus. You please wake up."

Eyes opened against my will, even though there was absolute nothing to see except total darkness. My eyes closed once again.

"Up," Tin told me.

"No," I sort of imagined saying.

"We cook breakfast. Right soon. Now! Mr. Hop always extra early start-up on first morning out. Hands eat five o'clock. Before cows put hinders in air to stand up."

Opening an eye, I saw Tin Pan.

"No," I said.

"Hah! You maybe fish for trouble. Bad. Bad. Mr.

Hopple make rules. Everybody eat early." Tin poked me with the blunt end of a large cookspoon. "Eat early. *Before cows up.*"

Again another jab. And this time twice. Nobody, I was thinking, even considers eating at midnight, or whatever it was.

"You shake up, you eat," Tin Pan informed me. "Ah, you no get up, help . . . no eat. Go hungry."

In a huff, Tin left.

Had he said four o'clock?

This much I'd reasoned out. On the cattle drive, only two watches were brought along. Mr. Hopple carried one. Who toted the other? Our smiling little Tin Pan.

Forcing myself to sit up on heartless turf, the agony of stiffness went shooting through my backbone; from there, into every tendon. In fact, muscles I didn't even own were throbbing. Between my legs, the Devil's Daughter still sort of balked and bucked and sundanced.

Micah then appeared.

"Morning, Tee. How be?"

"Asleep."

"Me too. Best you shake awake, baby bro."

"Why?"

Micah grinned. "Because I'm hungry. Golly, I could surround a dozen eggs, maybe leftover beef, and a bunch of Tin's biscuits."

"Now!" Tin reappeared, threatening the spoon at me, then adding some colorful non-English terms that didn't sound overly flattering.

Standing me to my feet, Micah said, "Tin wants you to slice bacon, in two fry pans. Then, when it's better'n halfway cooked, fetch out the pork bellies and drop eight dozen eggs into hot grease. He'll expect you to cook every egg because they won't keep another day in this heat."

Pulling on a all-night-stiff boot, I said, "Mrs. Krickitt doesn't do eggs like so."

Micah agreed. "But she ain't with us, Titus. We're not at the ranch. It's different out to here, brother, away from used-to. You wanted along. Well, you're here. And it's breakfast hour."

He walked away.

I sliced the giant rashers of pork belly bacon, butchered from the most prosperous hogs on Spur Box. The strips were lengthened into two fry pans the size of wagon wheels. Tin Pan's flame was low, flat, and evenly coaled, the right shape of a functional fire.

Micah had been right. The bacon got fished out. Then, into puddles of bubbling bacon fat, eggs got dropped. *Crack. Plop. Sizzle.* That was the first egg. Then a hundred others.

Tin Pan, leaving me alone, busied himself with

Dutch-oven biscuits, grits, and a few dozen fritters formed out of last evening's corn dodgers.

How, I mused, did he manage it? Our cook never wasted a crumb. Each speck of food, along with plenty of hot grease, was converted into solid nutrition for a dozen sturdy hands who faced a day's work few other men could endure.

As I stirred yellow and white into mounds of scramble, I remembered that it had been Mrs. Krickitt who had hired on Tin Pan. Our housekeeper probable informed Tin that cowhands got up early in order to store away everything edible in sight. This, I'd guess she told Tin, these men deserved; they enjoyed little else. No wives. No dances. A once-a-week blast in Dry Bone at The Bent Ace, an establishment caring little or naught for their merriment. Or health. Only to milk them of their money, and then, once they were broke, to hurry 'em out a alley door to make a place at the bar for fresh payrolls.

One by each, our cowhands (those who weren't a mile away, slumping in a saddle, watchdogging over hundreds of slumbering cows) began to shake out of damp blankets, stagger ten feet, and empty their bladders.

Some at each other.

This might have been their one and only rapturous feeling for an entire sunbaked, soil-devouring and saddle-spanking day.

Anyone watching had to admire Tin Pan.

Weasel quick, he darted everywhere to once, cooking and frying and piling bent plates high with hot predawn chow. His trio of coffeepots, available on three tiny fires, included a thick rag wrapped around each pot handle to prevent some sleepy hand from ruining his grip. When he wasn't heaping grub to a plate, Tin stirred his black kettle of grits.

Men ate in the dark around the cooking fires, mostly in groups. A few, having heard several repeats of Spout's and Bagpipe's no-quit conversation, ate alone.

Domino and Vinegar already had a discussion heated up, with Vin lecturing on the subject of a certain lady's undergarments.

"Tee, more eggs now." Our cook was still annoyed with me, and thus I wasn't Mr. Titus for a spell.

Tin Pan shouted faster than a counter gal at a short-order diner in Dry Bone, and I found myself moving near to nimble. Remembering yesterday, I understood why. On a cattle drive there's no noon meal. Once the cows git poked and prodded toward the railhead, it makes little sense to halt a moving herd. For men, it was eat only twice a day, making each meal something between a free-for-all feast and an outright battle.

Cowhands ate as though there'd never be another plate of hot chow beneath their chins. Biscuits were grabbed, devoured whole, and even stuffed into their stinking shirts (or musty saddlebags) for later consuming.

Tin and I were the only two who didn't hunker down to breakfast. We ate on a dead-hustle run.

Mr. Hopple, although first on his feet among the working hands, was last to pile a plate for himself. This had always been Hop's way. Mrs. Krickitt once remarked that Ornell was one part ramrod and two parts parent. True enough. Among the lowly laboring cowpokes of Spur Box, especially for the younger hands, our foreman ruled as both a rigid-strict father and caring mother. Ornell Hopple was the nearest thing to a drum major that a cattle rancher would brag. He knew each man. In addition, his mind could catalogue every hand's talents, as the instruments they played. On a cattle drive, a marching band, Ornell's baton seldom quit directing us men and animals.

I honest questioned if Hop ever slept.

Our direction was due east and then southeast, from near Naples, across the giant dangling toe of Florida, toward the railroad and slaughterhouse at Homestead. Because a herd requires water, we had to zigzag pond to pond. It wasn't a straight crow-fly line; instead, a snaking meander of far more than two hundred miles.

None of those miles conquered easy.

Also, I discovered, not a one of our five hundred

cows trusted any of us; each animal determined to try another route, retreat to Spur Box, or tour Alabama. My day started at four o'clock in the morning and persisted until way after sunset, at a time when the final fry pan had been scoured to Tin Pan's persnickety standards. By day's end, I didn't wash, undress, or even remove my boots.

Grabbing a blanket, I just melted to a lump of sleep. Drifting off, I imagined hearing the Cowboy Ghost mumble three words in a husky and exhausted voice.

"Ya done good."

CHAPTER THIRTEEN

Another day passed.

On the following noontime, Fitch, on a wet horse, came thundering toward Mr. Hop as though Satan himself were a hoof behind.

"Tribulation," he told Ornell.

Fitch Parmalee was recent from Carolina, newly signed on, and now (with the eyesight of youth) served as our point rider, scouting a far piece in front of the herd, reporting back to our foreman about unwalkable ground or anything pesky. Fitch, several Spur Box bunkhouse intellectuals maintained, had a *brain*. He could cipher a column of figures (without using fingers or toes), decode print, and once had read a entire dime novel.

Cover to cover!

Rarely did Fitch offer anything to say. He mere performed a job without cuss or comment. When he did speak up, however, Ornell Hopple reasoned that Fitch had possible cause and warranted a open ear.

Before explaining his panic, Fit wheeled his misty mare in a circle, then again, to settle her. A hard-rode stringer doesn't pull short, then stand at easy.

Dismounting, walking to where Ornell was also unhooking a leg off his gray gelding, Fitch bent to pick up a stick. Shielded behind a clump of low-growing palmetto, I sneaked my horse closer to eavesdrop. Without another word, Fitch scratched two six-foot lines in the sand, forming an X.

"Crossed lances," he told Ornell. "I'm new to Florida, but I bet today's pay they wasn't planted there by preachers."

"How far ahead?"

Fit shrugged. "Maybe two mile. One glance, and I hightailed it from yonder to here in a breath and a breather. Made me sweat my shirt wet through. Like I'd waded a swamp."

Ornell nodded. "Don't blame ya, Fitch. To see such, riding out there lonesome, is enough to curdle a man's blood."

"What's it mean, Mr. Hop?"

"That we're fixing to tramp across their territory, so the Seminole don't intend to afford us any hospitable."

"It ain't *theirs*." Fitch scowled. "Is it?"

Hop shook his head. "However, it certain ain't *ours*. And nobody's going to convince 'em such. Rightful used to be theirs, most of Florida, since away before them murderous Spainers come, crossing themselves and then butchering everyone else." He paused. "Fitch, if I had to venture into a mossy murk to inform some painted savage this ain't his honest range, I'd sooner need to change my drawers."

Though it was a steamer of a day, their conversation chased a chill up my backbone. And I felt my horse shudder.

"Mr. Hopple," Fitch asked him, "you cotton to whoa the cows?"

"Not dang likely." Removing his hat, Ornell swiped his sweating brow with a sleeve. "What we ought is to skirt bother. Avoid a head-on. Yet we gotta hustle five hundred beefs over the next twenty of their cussed Seminole miles. Ain't no U.S. Army here. Not since they abandoned Fort Dog, packed up their fevers, and vamoosed."

"You mean we're on our own?"

"Afraid so," Mr. Hop said. "Sometimes a best way to dodge mischief is not to crank it up."

Fitch reclimbed his mare. Then pointed ahead. "With all respect, Mr. Hop, you wasn't out there alone. And didn't see two feathered lances crossed in the sand. There was a third object I forgit to mention, lying on the dirt betwixt them two long sharp stickers."

"What was it?"

Fitch swallowed. "Mr. Hopple . . . it was a human skull."

To me, our foreman was starting to look older. More tired. Ornell was staring straight ahead, out across what appeared to be the endless sun-beaten stretch of a deserted Florida flat he had crossed and recrossed so many countless times. Treeless, with the exception of a few isolated clumps of cabbage palm, tall naked trunks, topped by a spiked ball of green fan fronds.

"They're out there," Hop said. "Looking at us right now. We could parade by a Seminole, a few foot distant, and never see his face. Only feel the sting of his knife." Hop spat. "But we won't turn our tails." His voice sounded a bit ragged at the edges.

"What'll we do, sir?"

"Bend a little, yet march straight on through, heads high, driving our cattle with us. And try our blessed best to appear as if we're *not* of the Spanic persuasion."

Fitch made a wry face. "Ain't the Seminole supposed to be living content on some sort of a federal reservation?"

Ornell forced a weary grin. "Son," he said, "if your people once was free Seminoles and git confined to reservations . . . how *content* would you be?"

"We sashay full ahead? Sort of?"

"The reservation's north. So we bend south, prior to hitting the swamp. Then north again. After that, southeast to Homestead."

"Right, Mr. Hop."

"Ride forward and turn our pointers, whoever they might be. Who's up there?"

"Vinegar and Domino. One more . . . Horrible."

"Okay, git started, Fitch. I'll be along. In a mile or so, if by chance our very first steer is meeting up with crossed lances, count on Vinegar not to spook. He's to waltz our cattle smack through that hurdle like it weren't present."

Fit circled his horse. "Got it."

"Fitch . . ."

"Yes, Mr. Hop."

"Continue to scout, up front. Unless, of course, you sudden got the balls of a mouse and can't abide peril."

Fitch Parmalee gulped. "I can cut it." Spurring the mare, Fit galloped due easterly, perhaps wondering if he could convince Tin Pan to swap jobs.

Unable to contain anxiety, my boots nudged a mount to overtake our foreman. At first, he looked a mite surprised that I'd appeared so sudden.

"Titus," Hop said calmly, as though wondering if

it was fixing to sprinkle, "you're supposed to be riding flank, with Spider. How come you're here? Better be a solid reason."

"Sorry." I sucked in a breath. "But I was wondering if we'd be meeting up any honest-to-goodness Seminole."

Our foreman stared at me. His eyes darkened, deepening into a inky midnight of absolute authority.

"Youngster, it don't concern one square inch of your confounded lily-white backside! If you flake off your duties once more, as you're doing now, I'll snatch you off'n that animal so fast your rectum will still be riding. And you'll hoof it home." Eyes narrowing, he spoke in a voice turned raspy. "If I report unmanly conduct to Mr. Mac, he'll quarantine you to a upstairs bedroom until your beard turns gray."

My lungs refused to exhale.

Mr. Hop pointed. As he done so, I noticed that his hand no longer seemed to hold steady. "Go back to your outside position. Else, by dang, you'll do naught for this drive except assist Tin Pan to peel onions or swab grease."

His words made me freeze.

"Git!" he spat.

Leaving at a gallop, I got to Spider in less than half a minute, collecting my mount, and thankful I'd escaped a full blast of punishment from our top hand.

Spider Shellenberger, all six foot six of him, rode dozing in the saddle as he'd rid midnight to dawn, on night watch.

His eyes popped.

"Tee," he asked hoarsely, "any news?"

"Nothing," I said, employing the wisest word, at the smartest time, that I'd final managed to gush out the entire day.

The itch to tell Spider about the up-ahead Seminoles was crawling all over inside my shirt worse'n hives. Or cattle ticks. Whatever, I held mum because my bare feet had stepped into enough brown trouble. So for the remainder of the flank shift, I allowed Spider to saddle slump and sleep while I chased the strays that wandered from our side of the herd. Not a one escaped. Hollering until hoarse, I managed to escort each gypsy back to the bunch.

According to both Spider and Bagpipe, it was usual proper to refer to animal groups as *a bunch of cows*, but a *band of horses*.

After helping Tin Pan fling food at everybody, I soaped pots, pans, plates, and plenty of forks to Tin's liking. Smiling, he smuggled me an extra-tender ear of buttery sweet corn, which I gnawed to cob in three seconds. Aware I no longer ate human. Rather like a homeless dog.

I lay down.

Prior to sleeping, I forced myself to review Mr. Ornell Hopple's warning and concluded he was right to chew on me. A man ought to rein himself in check. No way I could control a Seminole, so best I contain Tee MacRobertson. Closing my eyes, I mumbled the day's benediction.

"Curiosity is for Cleopatra."

CHAPTER FOURTEEN

✕☐

We bent our herd south.

For a entire day, every Spur Box eye alertly scanned the griddle-hot Florida flat lying ahead of us.

Our restless cows were bawling more often. Without cease. Instead of their usual mindless march toward Homestead and death, the animals hankered to scatter or turn back. Again and again, a cow would shy at a clump of palmetto, as though suspecting the greenery was masking a unknown threat, and scamper from the herd. By noon, all horses under saddles lathered white from the heat, the hustle, but mostly from the haunting in their eyes. Like the cows, the horses were also skittery. They knew something we didn't.

Mr. Hopple gave the order to work a horse for a quarter of the daylight instead of a half, and to retack three times, not just once.

This amounted to rest for horses, little for men.

"I can smell 'em," Vinegar said to nobody in particular, unaware that I was riding the Devil's Daughter close enough to overhear his concern. He forced a laugh. "And they probable smell *me*. Most folks can."

"What is it?" I asked.

The old puncher flinched. "Nothing. And believe me, Tee, I certain ain't rightful enjoying it."

The two of us were riding point, leading the bunch, because Fitch had been saddled for extra hours and had passed out inside Micah's tool wagon, his head on his saddle. As we rode ahead of the mass of bellowing beef, Vinegar kept squinting in one direction, then another, continually ragging his perspiring face with a soggy bandanna, which could no longer absorb. It merely rearranged Vin's sweat.

"Tee, I got me a foredoom. Up ahead. Can't see even a whisker of them sneakies. Yet they're yonder."

"What are they doing?"

"Waiting a chance, boy. Listening to the clanking rattle of Tin's wagon. They know where we all be and how we're headed. Trouble is, far as I know, we didn't bring no rifles. Maybe that's wise. Had we, them Seminoles would've done us by now. Done us dead. Left our skeletons to bleach pale under the sunshine." Vin sighed. "They won't use rifles to betray their positions. Just silent arrows. Or lances. At least the dang diggers ride into plainview."

Hearing what Vinegar Swinton was saying twisted my head from right to left and back again, seeing nothing. Yet imagining that I could spy a black-haired head, bound in cloth, soundless, with staring eyes.

"How far," I asked Vinegar, "do we still have to drive before we make it to Homestead?"

"Miles. We might be a day closer to the railhead than backwards to Spur Box. But I don't guess we're comfortable neighborly to either end."

"We're alone."

Vinegar nodded. "Isolate."

My throat tightened.

"Vin, is it this way on every cattle drive?"

He shook his head. "Naw. Years and years go by without a chickeny peep from red people. And then, without no warning, they git all bothersome and raise a ruckus. Most times, they reside quiet in the swamp, poling their dugouts over the silent water and through the ghostly greenery."

"Where do they live?"

Vinegar grunted. "No surveyor's ever drawed a accurate map about it. Know why? Because it don't remain the same. Always shifting. Land becomes water, and then the water dries to firm. There's bear, panther, deer . . . not to mention gators and snakes. I seen spiders bigger than a man's hand. Beaver, possum, otter, and raccoon. All manner of fish, freshwater oysters, and clams. And more turkeys than Thanksgiving."

We rode silent for a while as I waited for Vinegar to continue his description of the nearby territory.

"Well," I said, "sounds as though the Seminole Nation has plenty to eat. They certain don't require any of our Spur Box steers."

"Tribute," said Vinegar.

"What's that?"

Before answering, the old puncher wheeled his horse around to retain a large yearling calf that had decided to wander.

"It's a bribe," he said at last. "The Seminole maybe cogitate that us ranchers don't carry a right to cross their terrain unless we cough 'em up a forfeit. Maybe a steer or two for their stewpots."

"And they expect our tribute? Our cows?"

"Betwixt you and me, Titus, I preference we surrender a cow than a cowhand." Vinegar spat. "Mr. Hopple don't glimpse it such. He don't buy friendship. We're driving five hundred, and our foreman counts on delivering not a single animal less. Hop won't appease people. Red or white. Mr. Mac wouldn't condone even the offer of a cow's fart, no less a entire cow." Vinegar winked at me. "Nor your grandfather, Mr. Maxwelton. Thrifty men. Tighter than a bull's ass in fly time."

Saying nothing, I rode quietly along at Vinegar Swinton's knee, as I'd done for so many years on Spur Box. Now, however, neither of us was to home.

It made me turn up my shirt collar.

Vinegar noticed. "You chilly?"

"No."

Vin snorted a doubt. "Well, I be. Death's a cold customer. Frigid and final, no turning around to try again."

"Aw, come on, Vin. We're not fixing to *die*, are we? Not here. Because we are not living in Grandfather's time. This is 1924. It's today!"

Vinegar pulled in his roan, turned, and then stared straight at me. His eyes turned to ice. "Yes," he said. "And I want my tomorrow."

Before I could answer, eager to kid Vinegar Swinton about being afraid, something forced me to remain mute. A noise. It was foreign to any sound that I'd ever heard, a rattle, as though someone was clacking rocks together. Not quite. The noise was being created by hollow objects, meeting, then echoing. At first, it was a single pair of clackers. Then a second. In a minute's time, the air became filled with clattering. Dry and deadly. It came from a long way off.

"What is it, Vinegar?"

"Don't guess I ought to tell you."

"You do know?"

He nodded. "Absolute. A decade ago, I heard the same sound. Took a while to figure out what caused it."

"Nothing human."

"Wrong."

Looking at Vin, I asked him the silent question because I had to know the answer. Had to! Even though the expression on the puncher's face announced that he'd prefer to stay still.

"Bones," he said.

As he spoke, more and more rattles started to capture the distant air, commanding our attention.

"Animal bones, right?"

"Not hardly. Human bones, Tee. They'll make that sound to worry us sick." Vinegar spat. "Bones serve the Seminole same way that bagpipes do for the Scottish. Bones and bagpipes don't actual kill. All they do is drive the enemy out of mind. And territory."

I said nothing, wanting to hear more.

"Miccosukee, some call themselfs," Vin said, as we rode along. "Maybe a certain breed of Seminole or a separate tribe. I ain't sure. Possible the warriors rattle them bones. Maybe not."

"Who else would?"

"Their women and little ones. I don't guess we'll see a warrior. They can hide in trees, below ground, and under all them shallow ponds of black water. No, we won't see 'em, Tee. What we'll see is fewer of our cows every day. Maybe fewer *us*."

We rode silently, both of us listening to the echo of bone rattles, a distant and hostile chattering, spoken by the bones of the dead.

Vinegar pointed to the sky. "Up ahead," he told me, "us Spur Boxers got more'n one problem. See that purple? Never knowed it to fail. It's a storm. Not just in front of us neither. It'll flood the entire state."

Looking where Vinegar was pointing, I saw the darkening ahead, and also to the north and south.

The cows noticed. Anytime prior to a rain, there's only one thing a cow will do before the storm hits. She'll lie down, in advance, to ensure having a dry place. She won't wait until the ground is soggy. Lying down early provides a bed that remains dry and warm.

Cows stalled in their tracks. Not moving, just standing still and attempting to lie, until one hand or another rode up close enough to lash a red hide with a loosely coiled rope. Vinegar was performing this service. So was I. But with little result. The bunch was mere budging.

Slower and slower.

The front hoofs of my horse slightly stumbled on a prone cow. Strange, but the cow never even twitched. Just rolled on her side without blinking.

Then I spotted the arrow.

CHAPTER FIFTEEN

E asy," said Vin.

Looking around, I saw Vinegar and Horrible attempting to heft up cows that had decided to bed down. With little success. Cows lay everywhere, ditto rode shouting men.

"Soft," I told myself. "It's only one arrow, and a single dead cow, so don't loose your head about it. Rein steady."

I forced myself calm. This became increasingly difficult as other dead beefs (each with the stern end of a protruding arrow) were being discovered in our herd. Although not actual counting, my brain tallied over a score of slaughtered steers. What made it so eerie was that none of us saw even the first Seminole. We all witnessed the dead cattle.

Ornell rode to us at a crisp canter.

"Keep 'em moving, boys. But stay mounted. I don't want nobody on foot amongst a bunch that's threatening to spook mad. A steer'll sniff danger in one breath." He looked ahead at the purpling sky. "Head 'em east, in the face of that electric storm. And please, nobody decide to stay dry beneath a tree. Unless you're eager to turn into toast."

He rode off.

Thunder kept rumbling. Cows in a panic. All of us were hooting out urgings to the herd until our throats sawed raw.

As the first drop of rain stung my face, lightning near blinded, and an immediate crash of thunder muffled me deaf for a few seconds. The rain increased into a gray misty sea of water. A shard of lightning struck a nearby pine, turning the drenched tree into a giant burning torch.

Cows rambled off in every direction.

"Hold 'em together," Vin was screeching at me and Horrible. "Spread out wide, to work a big circle around the beefs. Nose 'em back to center."

On our right, the pine, like a great orange god, blazed and crackled more ferociously, spooking the cattle away from it, turning most of our cows due north.

Toward the Seminole.

Doing what Vinegar told me, I rode my horse into

the wide circle of riders. Or so I guessed. Little or no visibility to guide me. Add to that another problem: The horse, ears lying flat toward me, was becoming more unruly with every flash of static. The light, noise, rain, yelling men, and bawling cattle did little to settle her to obedience. She buckled frisky, twisting to one side, then another, rearing, striking out at the storm with front hoofs.

Half a dozen cows charged into us, knocking my mount off balance. Down we both tumbled. On impact with the ground, the mare grunted, probable with as much panic as pain. No horse ever wants to lose footing, because its escape route to safety depends on four solidly planted legs.

Even though we hit a yielding mud, the sudden agony in my knee was unbearable. I was certain my leg got busted. Somehow, as the mare struggled to her feet, my body stayed clamped to the saddle.

"*Stick,*" I thought I heard my Cowboy Ghost holler. "Git throwed, you might die. Your leg's not broke. If so, you'd know it."

So I stuck.

As the rain was stinging my eyes, I tried to squint a look at where my mare was going. Wherever it was, we'd arrive sudden soon. With a high shrill nicker of fear, my horse bolted, smashing into the slower cows and jumping over the beefs that slipped down. So I had to turn her. Neck-rein her to circle. Get the cows to mill tight. They'd be a lot safer crowded than loose.

The storm thickened.

In such a situation, each man and every animal is alone. My world boiled into a underwater Hell of maddened sky and muddy earth. Though it was daytime, it was nevertheless darker and deeper than any night I'd ever known. The noise wouldn't quit. Horses and beefs created a continual deafening din that caused my brain to spin.

How I wanted to be back home.

"Mrs. Krickitt!" I yelped.

Only once. And then reason somehow muffled my repeating her name. Doing so had been folly.

"Micah!"

A single time I had to call his name, because saying it, or thinking it, strengthened me. Always had. That's the way of it when a skinny kid owns a tree for a brother.

Years ago, Mrs. Krickitt had warned me, in a scholarly tone, about the Heavenly wrath of an Old Testament God. I didn't understand. So our housekeeper explained it: "Nature," she said. "When our blessed Mother Nature corrects us, she acts violently. Be it a earthquake, tidal wave, or volcano spittle. Nature's adjustments are usual massive, beyond our comprehension in magnitude and might. When our Earth demands a fixing, the Almighty allows Mother Nature to smite us, wielding a heavy hammer."

"Why?" I'd asked her.

Mrs. Krickitt had smiled and touched my hand. "To remind us mortals, Titus Timothy, that it is not *we* frail things who are supreme."

Around me, at the moment, Surpremity now clubbed Earth and every Earthling with unrelenting force. Electricity. Clamor. Wet. Destruction and confusion captured us and commanded our rapt attention. There existed no customary haven of *indoors*. We were naked, unarmed, totally unprepared for such an attack by a tumultuous trio of elements: voltage, thunder, and rain. Under this, a man could be mashed into mud like a tent peg. Crippled. Killed at will.

There was no guiding my horse. With every twitch of her muscular head and neck came the urge to loosen my grip on the reins, grab the saddle horn, and pray. Somehow I contained her. I owed her control, and guidance.

There seemed no way to dominate the mare. Beneath me, between my thighs, she'd reverted back to being barbarous. A mad mustang. She brought to mind my sixteenth birthday, a rope, and my baptism, along with

Micah's words: "Father," he'd warned during that heated afternoon tilt in the corral against the broomtail, "is bound to start looking your way. And *expecting*."

I'd show him. Expectation or no. My fingers tightened on the wet leather ribbons of the bridle. The weakness hardened to strength.

"Come on, girl," I said to the mare. "You're no more scared than I am, so let's circle cows. That's our job. It's time we earned our oats."

For too many years, I decided as I heeled the mustang mare ahead in rain, I'd been our outfit's little pet. Mrs. Krickitt's hair-slicked hobby. Well, it dang ought to change, and whistle a new tune.

"Git 'em, Tee."

As I tried to circle, a couple of strays cut in front of my mare and me, possible intending to vacation in Key West. With a confident nudge to the mare, I charged forward to bump the gypsies around, changing both their intent and direction, guiding them toward territory with the most cow cries.

Growing up in Florida, I'd witnessed electric storms aplenty, but none with the savagery of this one. My ears went total deaf after one brutal crack. Yet, even in the blinding tropical torrent of rain, I managed somehow to hear another horror.

Above the head-hammering noise, another sound. Hoofs. My old Cowboy Ghost whispered only one word of warning.

"Stampede."

CHAPTER SIXTEEN

✶☐

The animals charged as one.

Every cow and unsaddled horse bolted, knowing not where to go, scattering as would husks of hay in a hurricane. The sky darkened to a chilling afternoon midnight, offering us mortals a possible preview of how a world might end: in a deluge of demonic destruction. Beneath me, a heated horse was tiring, and I felt the persistent caldron of her overworked body.

"Tee." It happened to be Vinegar Swinton who had yelled. He turned his mount. "Where ya been?"

"Circling the herd, the way you said."

"Stout lad. Keep to it," he shouted through the driving rain. "Turf's soggy, so the beefs'll poop out sooner."

"Okay."

"Stay wide, boy. Outside the bunch. If you're trapped inside it, your teeth might be eating a horn.

Them steers git to processing over half a ton apiece. So wary yourself. Hear?"

"I hear, Vin. Thanks."

He rode off into mist.

Hard to say how long the storm persisted. It continued to prod us and pound us into a muddy mire. But then, as it had abruptly begun, the weather clicked itself off to quit. The sun shined. As dark sky lightened and cleared, there was nothing to behold except a monster of a mess. For miles. Spent cows stood sentry still, panting heads drooping almost to rest their foaming muzzles on an exhausted Florida.

"Titus!"

Turning, I saw Mr. Hop, considerable damp, and appearing at least a decade older than when I'd last seen him. After a check of his gelding, he gave me three instructions, holding up fingers.

"Ride around and give me a head count. First, all the men. Second, the condition of our two wagons, Micah's and Tin Pan's. Third, a thumbnail tally on how many horses stuck with us. My guess, even if some spooked away fearful, they'll eventual return, because we brung enough oats to serve as a tether."

"Will do, Mr. Hop."

"Let the beefs rest wherever they took a notion to stop. It's the men, wagons, and mounts we blessed need to persist us toward Homestead." He looked at the western sky. "Less'n an hour of daylight left, so git riding. Pronto."

"I'm off."

Studying my horse, Mr. Hopple made a face. "Tee . . . why in the deuce of damnation did you bargain for that mangy hunk of buzzard bait you're aboard on?"

"She's my favorite," I said. "Out of pity, because none of the other hands can rope her, or *stick*. We call her Devil's Daughter."

Our foreman shook his head. "Yup, I recognize that unshod shoddy. She's the banger that rid her spine of Spider before he could work up a yahoo."

I grinned. "If it'll help, I'd be willing to give Spider a few pointers on how to avoid cartwheels in midair."

Leaving Mr. Hopple's opinionated jaw dropping in respectful dismay, I spun the Devil's Daughter a crisp one-eighty and galloped off. Back yonder at Spur Box, there haven't been many waddies able to squeeze in a final dig at Ornell.

I final located Tin Pan. Although commenting about our delightful Florida weather, Tin was busily sorting food supplies, including oats for the horses, and discarding wet flour and salt. Luckily, the vegetables and oranges were rainproof, able to continue southeast.

Dismounting, I said, "Tin, thanks for being alive."

"You. Me too. Very bad things. Night sky in day-time. You find all us peoples in a safe place?"

"That's my job. Where you keeping the carrots? My horse could use a bunch. Okay if I reward her? She's fixing to crumple."

Tossing me a corsage of orange vegetation, Tin Pan watched me hand-feed my animal, with a look of suspicion. He sneered at my mare. That's our world. Everybody's got to spot someone lower to look down on.

"Broomtail," he said, as an insult.

"Used to be. This ol' gal is proving out a willing animal. Not for the entire outfit. Only for me." I grinned at our cook. "Got any oats handy?"

Tin scooped a measure of semidry oats into my hat, which served as a feedbag. My mare bit into the oats as if never fed since her weaning. As she chawed, yellow-green drool leaked from her lips to my hat. Not caring, I wiped her muzzle, using my sleeve, and spoke to her softly.

"Feel better, sweetheart?"

Tin Pan, however, was still disapproving. "Broomtail," he repeated. "Mustang mutt. Better use as dog meat."

Maybe I was tired, ornery, or just plain fed up with weather and an endless day of cowpoking. Chalk it up to temper. So I whistled off steam. "That's right, Tin. But she's a finer horse than *you'll* ever ride." With that, I rode off to find Micah, trying to cuss in Chinese.

Finding him wasn't pretty. In the storm, his mules must have bolted, as the tool wagon had shifted in mud, overturned, and pinned my brother underneath its mass, helpless and alone. Micah's shirt was soaked black with blood

Kicking out of the saddle, I rushed to him.

His moon smile met me, as though he'd been waiting for this moment. Instead of being self-concerned, Micah pointed at his mules. Both were helplessly floundering in a mire, unable to regain any footing. Each mule was sawing for help in a hideous mulish cry. Every bray sounded closer to strangulation.

"Tee," my brother told me, "cut 'em loose." He paused to fight for breath under the weight of his tack wagon. "There's a knife in the boot. Go locate it. Before they kick one another to death, cut 'em unharnessed."

As Micah said, I found a knife. The first mule loosened easily. The second, however, worked up a panic and then planted a hoof into my giblets that threatened to stop the world. Leastwise, all breath. But then, instead of slashing her throat, I sliced enough leather thongs to free her.

Both mules left in a hurry, their collars trailing long whipping hitches of leather.

Returning to my brother, a closer look informed me

132

that he was worse off than earlier. More drained of blood. The ruddy face was ashen. Blue eyes now an icy gray, as though preparing to occupy some arctic resting place in which there was no longer a warmth of living.

"I'll move the wagon off you, Micah. I can do it." But thrusting against it failed. Still, I pulled until I felt my bowels move. My head pounded. The wagon wouldn't budge; so, in a fury, I beat at it with my fists. My fingernails tried to tear it apart.

"I'll go fetch help. So we can save you."

Micah shook his head. "Too late. I feel cold."

His words stabbed into me. "Micah, please don't quit." Bending closer, I said, "Ranchers can't die away from home."

"You," he said, "are the next rancher now."

"No. I'm not listening up."

His fingers grabbed my shirt to quiet my panic. "Best you do." Micah's hand rose to my face. "Soon," he said, "you'll be sprouting a beard. Don't allow our guys to chide you about it. Just razor it off. Allow yourself time." His eyes faded to glassy. "Can you hear me? Patience."

I nodded.

"Father," he said quietly, "always expected me to . . ."

"I know, Micah. I've always known. You weren't born to be another Rob Roy MacRobertson. Nor was I.

Father never understood either of us. Maybe not our mother. Perhaps not himself."

"You've growed, Titus. You growed up about a year in only a few brutal days."

I held his hand. "Not enough. But I owe you, big brother. And I'll make good my debt. Understand what I'm talking about?"

His voice sounded weaker. "The ranch is our purpose, Titus. Our destiny as MacRobertsons. We both know. Father didn't have to drill duty into us. Or pile on extra weight."

"What happened, Micah? Something did. Years ago, when I was still too young to comprehend, it took place. And I have to know about it. Now."

His grip on my fingers tightened to almost unbearable. The sudden strength was normal. Plants, just prior to wilting into death, somehow manifest the will to bloom.

"You were seven," he said.

"Was it the Sunday I got my Bible?"

Micah nodded. "On that sorrowful afternoon, I got bare-knuckle beaten by a Mr. Greer O'Ginty. Whipped to a bloody heap. Father felt only his own regret. Never my hurt. Our guests left, and then Father got raging drunk, in despair, unable to face the shame of his son's defeat."

"I sort of remember that."

"By the time Father passed out cold, Mrs. Krickitt was already upstairs in my room and icing my swollen face. She held me in her arms, rocking me like a newborn."

"I wish I'd done it for you too."

His body trembled. "In your Bible, read the fourth chapter of Micah . . . about swords and plowshares." His speech became a whisper. "I'm the pounded sword, Titus. You're a plowshare that begins a happier harvest."

"Somehow," I said, "I'll bring you to the ranch."

"No! Plant me where I lie. Please don't cart my body back to Spur Box. Understand? I want free of him. Here I'll be at liberty from my twenty-nine years of Hell."

He said no more. Open blue eyes stared unblinking at a sunset, perhaps seeing where he was going. Micah Samson MacRobertson had begun another journey.

To a gentler home.

CHAPTER SEVENTEEN

✳☐

A spade. A split handle.

It was after sundown. Why was I recalling Mr. Hopple's tossing a useless spade out of the tool wagon, back at Spur Box? It seemed a century ago. But tonight I had to bury a brother. Exhausted, I was tempted to ride ahead to the herd in order to get help; but no, I wouldn't allow myself such a wilt of weakness.

Micah wasn't *their* brother.

He was *mine*.

Sorting through an assortment of gritty hardware inside the wagon, I sudden blessed Domino. He had listened to Mr. Hop's advice and then added a solid-handled shovel.

This I busied to move dirt and more dirt, to extract Micah's body from beneath a tack wagon that still lay crippled on its side. Two wheels up and two wheels down. With no mules. There wasn't a glimmer of visibility. Only half a moon. Enough to scrape away dirt, scoop upon scoop, to dig Micah clear.

Then, a problem.

Micah was too massive for me to move. Try as I would, there was no resulting budge, because of his ponderous proportions.

"Devil's Daughter," I told my animal, "it's been a dreadful long day for you and also for me." I patted her sweaty neck. "However, I'm fixing to ask a final task out of you, an extra tug. How come?" I leaned my exhausted face to hers. "On account I'm sort of still a kid and can't yet manage a full dose of manhood."

Saying no more, I used part of the shredded harness that the mules had vacated to hitch my mare to my brother. Instead of hooking a leg up into the saddle, I remained grounded in order to pull alongside her. Two of us, in harness. Yoked oxen.

"Heave," I commanded. "Git up, horse. Pull. Because if you don't, the both of us miserable critters are going to be stuck out here all night. So give gumption."

Bless her angular body. She pulled. My heart nearly stopped when the wagon lurched, teetering as if to roll on me. Then, with a groan, settled back.

My pony partner and I somehow performed, summoning a final ounce of energy left between us, and dragged my brother's body out from under the tool wagon. With my arms around her ugly old face, I kissed her hairy cheek, thanking her.

"Your part's ended." As I began to dig a grave with the shovel, I told my mount, "You stand there and supervise. Okay? Because, you see, this gentleman isn't your kin. He's mine. He is my bro. And nobody ever had better than Micah."

The grave was well over six foot long, two foot wide, and as deep as I had strength enough to spoon it. My last few shovelfuls of wet earth were little more than a paltry few grains of damp sand. Deep enough? Well, it would have to suffice, as the scrawny body of T. T. MacRobertson had no more to offer. Painful though it was, I managed to roll Micah's cold body into the fresh grave. He fell with a thud. This would be the last thing we'd share together. How could I make it significant? What does a half-growed kid do in the night to sanctify so limitless a loss?

Then, there it all come.

Again I was seven.

It was a late Sunday morning, back from church in Dry Bone with Mrs. Krickitt, and I was jumping on

Micah's bed. On him. Sporting a new Bible, being quiet, basking in his strength as he read a chapter to me. What was it?

"Isaiah," I told the night. Make yourself remember the dreadful day that you've always forced yourself to forget. Hear it now, Titus, as you reverently heard it then.

Determination brought it back.

"Because I knew," Micah had read to me, *"that thou art obstinate, and thy neck is an iron sinew . . ."*

A brother's deep voice of nine years ago slowly faded into faint recollection before sinking into darkness.

The dirt covered all of him. Except his face. Then, after I kissed his cold cheek, it too yielded to Florida sand. A mound, way above ground level, was left . . . darker earth, atop the dryer and blonder soil of the surface. My shovel patted it into a hill of silent dignity. Was this all I would have to honor him? This sad dome?

"Micah."

How should I tell Mr. Hopple? For that matter, the Spur Box cowhands who had accepted my brother into their midst, that exclusive clan of cowpokes, all of whom judged a man's performance far above pay or personality. Kneeling close to his grave, head bowed, my mind repeated what Micah Samson MacRobertson had never become.

Not another Rob Roy.

"And my vow to you, brother, is this: I, Titus Timothy MacRobertson, won't become another Rob Roy either. So rest your spirit."

There was feeble ability to rise, regain my feet, to stomp both of my boots into a yielding Florida turf to announce that no storm would defeat me. Only an hour or so ago, perhaps two, I'd witnessed the face of our foreman. Hop wore a look of yesterday. Yet still able to command cowhands, the kind to eat cactus, piss rattlesnake poison, and then coddle cows in night duty, sing 'em asleep with an alertness that would maintain our outfit, year after year and summer upon season.

News of Micah's death would hit Ornell hard.

At the moment, however, all I could do was fall on Micah's fresh-dug grave, allowing my cheek to feel the Florida sand that had become his blanket. My fingers gripped the gravel.

"Micah," I said, my eyes closing, "I'll somehow make you proud."

The night won.

When I awoke, darkness, except to the east, where a lengthy snake of predawn light stretched across the horizon's cabbage palms, promising a fresh day. And like every morning, a challenge to combat. As I moved my leg, a nicker. Opening an eye, I saw Florida's ugliest and most dutiful broomtail bronc. There she stood, in an uncharacteristic pose, one of almost regal dignity: my Devil's Daughter.

She hadn't run away. She'd stuck.

Knowing not what to do, I pulled off my hat, which still was stinking of oats and horse drool, and pushed it toward her.

"Here," I said. "You're my partner."

She snorted. Then, as I had hoped, leaned toward my hat.

"Thanks for not loping away in the night. Because I don't exact realize where we are. Right. And also thank you for helping me to bury . . . Micah." Saying his name cut me. "Come here, horse." Holding out a hand, I said, "Please. Right sudden now. On account I'm too drained to stand like a man."

In the east, a new dawn stretched and strengthened, then began to brighten into day. The Devil's Daughter sniffed my face.

"Bless you." I grinned at her, and possible she at me. "That's the last honest time I'll paint you so sorry."

As my hand touched her soft velvety muzzle, her

throat nickered softly. Then, a second noise. The voice of a Cowboy Ghost, advising me. There was a day's work waiting. And a competent foreman's orders to harken and obey.

I best go report to Mr. Hopple.

CHAPTER EIGHTEEN

Where," asked Vinegar, "ya dang keeping?"
Right then, and right there, the urge to tell
Vin about Micah's death and burial was near
too burdensome to bear.

"Circling" was all I said.

Vin dismounted.

I painful unfolded off Daughter, no more Devilish,
pulling off my saddle, and started to rub this loyal friend
dry. Vinegar Swinton rattled toward me on bowed legs
that weren't designed for hiking, but to clamp a cowboy
on the barrel of a bronc.

His eyes appeared wet, and shiny sad.

"Tee . . . it's Mr. Hop. Best you fetch Micah."

"Why?"

"Well, he's now gotta be *the man*, to take charge
of our drive." He spat a dry nothing from his mouth,

needlessly wiping his gray-stubble face with a dirty sleeve. It was rare to see Vinegar with no tobacco and little spit. "We need Micah right sudden. Where's he at?"

Vin's news gradual hit me.

But then to support all he'd been efforting to tell me, Vin added, "Mr. Hop's heart give out. Nothing us waddies could do to revive him. So we buried him proper. Domino said a few Bible words over the grave. You know, to help decent it all."

My hand stopped rubbing my horse. "I'm truly sorry." Saying it sounded so lame and so feeble, but the night alone had wrung me dry of grieving.

"Reckon you would be. Hop was genuine leather." Vin paused. "But now it'll be Micah bossing the outfit, clear to Homestead and back."

"No," I said. "It can't be my brother."

Vinegar scratched his lousy hair.

"Come again?" he asked me.

Breathing deep, and then releasing all of the air as though it was poison gas, I stared at our most capable cowhand and gave him the level honest.

"It's not to be Micah."

Vin squinted. "Tee, maybe you don't listen up good. Mr. Hopple is dead, boy. He's put underground. Nobody's here to ramrod, except one. And that's your bro."

Slowly I shook my head, keeping my hands moving on the mare so's they wouldn't tremble. "Micah's dead. He's also buried, a mile back yonder. Last night I dug his grave and covered him." I swallowed. "We don't have a Micah anymore."

"No!" said Vin, refusing to believe it.

I nodded.

"Tee . . . I can't find words to say. If'n I could, you know what they'd be." Vinegar looked all around, as if dazed. "I teached our little Micah to fork a horse. Long long ago." Vin shook his head. "Well, s'pose out of respect, we ought to round what head we can locate and turn ourselfs to home."

"*No*, we will *not*."

Vinegar whapped his hat against his leg. "Aw, come on, Tee . . . there ain't a sensible nohow we can keep a-going. Nope. We best make for Spur Box."

Raising a hand, I said, "Wrong, Mr. Swinton."

"But we don't got a foreman."

"Wrong again. As certain as my name is Titus Timothy MacRobertson, I am taking full charge of my cattle."

"You?"

"Me." I slapped the mare's rump to nudge her along a step, so I'd stand boot to boot against Vinegar. "Go tell the men. Tin Pan cooks up good grub and I offer fair

145

wages. Plus," I added, "a bonus of ten dollars a man when we reach Homestead. On top, an extra five apiece when we get back home together."

Vin appeared doubtful. "What'll Mr. Mac say to that?"

With the tip of my finger tapping Vinegar's chest, I told him the truth. "If our outfit promises, it pays." I let that sink in. Then, another gentler finger on Vin's damp excuse for a shirt. "Has a MacRobertson ever lied to you, Mr. Swinton?"

He thought for only a second.

"Not a once."

Pointing at my own puny chest, I said, "Nor will this one." Trouble is, I didn't quite think what to say next, until I remembered Mr. Hop's final order to me. So I passed it along. "Vin, here's what you're to do. I'll need a head count of the men. And horses. Pronto! Inform Tin Pan that he's to reward each returning horse or mule with oats. The cattle are too tuckered to stray. In one hour, we're all to meet at the chucky, where Tin Pan will prepare us a hearty hello."

"Then what?"

I grinned. "We parade to Homestead like a brass band."

Vinegar stared at me as though unable to believe that this little kid he'd always played roping with had sudden become his boss.

"Git going," I told him. "Bring me horses, and never mind bunching the cows. After we put our paunches outside some hot chow, we head southeast. Clear?"

"Clear."

Hooking a leg across a tired horse, he trotted off, too gentle a man to rowel rake a spent animal. After looping a fresh mount, a liver chestnut gelding, I saddled him, then kicked into an easy canter to where I figured I'd last seen Tin Pan. There he stood, beside his team of mules, Right and Wong, and also the two loose mules that had pulled the tool wagon. Micah's team. Made no sense to return to Micah's wagon and attempt repair. Besides, we needed a new double-mule harness.

"Tee?"

"I'm here." I kicked off the gelding. "In one hour, Tin Pan, we're going to feed all the punchers. I'll help you."

"What do for food? Rain spoil."

"Beef. There's plenty of fallen steers around here. So we cut up one of them. You'll probable find arrows in some."

Tin Pan shuddered. "Seminole." He spat. "Seminole people very bad. Awful, awful. Kill. Kill. Kill. Bad guys."

"Tin, stop and consider. The Seminole didn't put even *one* arrow through any of us. Only into steers. Because we crossed what they consider as their land.

They're not killers, Tin. All they are is proud."

"Bad people."

"Think whatever you notion. As for me, I'm leaning a mite more toward steak and grits. We'll soon be entertaining bellies so empty they echo, so let's hustle up."

"You not a boss."

"Wrong. Or as you say, Wong. I am very much the boss. Because Mr. Hop is dead, and so is my brother. Micah is dead, Tin. I'm in charge. And mind your manners, for if you fail to, upon returning back to Spur Box, I shall report to Mrs. Krickitt on your behavior. Best you realize the tongue-lash she'll fire in your direction." I paused. "Cross her, and she'll eat your marigolds. And then *you*."

Without further words, Tin and I located arrowed beef, dressed, and cooked it, offering it to all of our hungry hands. Along with plenty of coffee or tea plus a boiled turnip and a orange for everyone.

Never had I seen, or heard, our punchers eat with such solemnity. There were no fistfights, little conversation. Worthy of a church meeting. Vinegar, no doubt, had explained to them about Micah. His death, on top of Mr. Hopple's, was a double deal of bad cards, and perhaps more than a cowhand could hold. There was a chance some might quit.

Vin presented me with a formal report on our horses and mules. All four mules had survived. One horse had been arrowed, and another three had run away during the thunderstorm.

They had not yet returned.

"From now on," I told the men, "I'll expect all horses not under saddle to take a walking hobble. We'll be needing every one. Some of you will have to ride mules. Tin Pan tells me that not a manjack among us will go hungry, even though you'll be sick to silly of beef by the time this outfit lopes, or limps, into the place we're going. And that's Homestead. Nowhere else."

There was a rumble of doubt.

"Vinegar," I asked our senior, "did you tell the boys about a bonus? If so, there's no sense repeating."

Vin shook his head. "Nope. Didn't git around. So maybe you'd cotton to whistle the tune."

I told the hands about the bonus. Ten dollars at Homestead and then another fiver when we return home.

"Home." I repeated the word. "A dry bunkhouse and a cot that's not rained on, plus a variety of vittles that isn't always beef and grits. Spur Box is my home. And if you gentlemen stick with me, she'll be yours. Long as you hanker to hang loyal. If not, ride off right sudden and don't look back."

Nobody spoke.

At that moment, I suspected that I'd failed as a foreman. My one uppercut at manhood had crumpled into little more than a kid trying to rough up rowdies.

"Y'all," I said, "have lost Mr. Hop. So have I. Plus losing a brother. But remember this and recall it always. Micah and Ornell wouldn't have wanted us to hightail, to retreat to the ranch. So, as of now, this outfit will drive a bit more than cattle to Homestead." I looked at all of their faces. "With us we take along the spirit of two Spur Boxers: Ornell Hopple and Micah Samson MacRobertson. I won't ask you to honor *me*. Not yet. But for your own respect, cinch up and honor them."

With a quick squat, I hunkered down between Bagpipe and Spout to take one more sip of bitter coffee. Saying Micah's name had pounded me like a punch.

That's when Vinegar Swinton took over, casually flanked by Domino and Bug Eye, as though Vin had sired them by way of brood cows.

"Boys," said Vin, "we lost a plenty when we surrendered up Hop and Micah to the Lord. But right here, we sudden got us a leader. Who don't shave." He laughed. "Manhood ain't measured by size or age. Only in spunk. I never request nothing out of your lousy like. Until now. Think on it, fellers. This young man reppersents more'n a MacRobertson family. Who's he be?" Vin thumbed over his shoulder, to the northwest. "He's *home*."

"Thanks," I told Vinegar.

"Ya dang welcome, Mr. Titus."

CHAPTER NINETEEN

☒

The cowdiggers showed. But kept a hundred yards off.

They were only three, riding spent horses and looking storm tired; the two younger men were toting rifles, sideways, just behind their saddlehorns. The third was a chubby old codger with a white beard who established himself as the ringleader.

"We's don't want no trouble," his voice scraped at Bagpipe and me. "Just fixing to borrow twenty head of yo' steers and git lost."

Bag's tooth had been hurting, and he wasn't enjoying the merriest of moods. He spat in their direction. Before he could holler a retort, negotiations were cut short by a earsplitter of a *clang-clang-clang* from our chucky, a result of Tin's gonging a fry pan with a spoon. He motioned to me.

I wheeled my horse to face him

"Mr. Titus, we got surprise for digger men. I bring rifle and scattergun in wagon, like Mr. Mac order."

After Tin gave me the shotgun, Bag, our best marksman, rode up to snatch the rifle.

"Take careful," Tin said. "Loaded."

The rifle I recognized as my father's Winchester repeater. My scatter, an ancient Texas Ranger twelve-gauge long barrel, made for Montgomery Ward, was a usual inhabitant of our bunkhouse. A relic a old Cowboy Ghost might have used in years past.

Bag shouted to the three pukers who had reined their horses to a halt. "We're heavy armed. You hunks of crap'll be lucky if'n ya git half a cold cow turd off'n our outfit. Besides, we got you saddle tramps outnumbered, four to one, so best y'all turn tail. Unless you're fixing to sink next time you swim."

Tin Pan had been threatening them with a large skinner knife, its blade shining silvery in the sun. A cow-digger, who perhaps thought it was the glint of a rifle barrel about to aim, fired. A bullet whined off the chuck-wagon's tailgate, just missing our cook, who dived for cover.

Bag fired the Winchester. Five times.

In pain, a digger grabbed his shoulder, bending in the saddle. He and the oldtimer turned away, but the third man shot at us once and fled. Something hot hit me hard, and I turned sick with the hurting.

"Yeller bellies," Bagpipe yelled after them. Turning to me, his entire face became a silent scream. Yanking up my stained shirt, Bagpipe winced. "Tee, you caught it sorry."

Dismounting, holding my gut, I somehow managed to crawl inside Tin's chucky. Bag followed.

"What you want I should do, Mr. Titus?"

"Fetch it out."

Bag flinched. "But it's a bullet. You'll require a medicine doctor. Honest, you ought." He shrugged. "Please, don't go asking me about surgery stuff, on account I don't know how to read. Or think. All I knowed, Mr. Titus, is that a dang digger pumped a slug to your middle."

"Bag," I told him through clenched teeth, "listen up. Nobody, except maybe Vinegar, is to discover I been hit." I grabbed his shirt collar. "Between you, me, and Tin Pan. Savvy?"

He nodded. "Gotcha, Mr. Titus."

The way he said it heartened me.

"Light a fire," I said.

"Why?"

Feeling a hard plank beneath my head as I lay flat, I

said, "Because you're to snake it out of me. Right here. Now. Nobody else needs know." I glared at him. "This is prime."

"What's that?"

"Means that what I'm telling you is more important than anything. Got it? So fire up a flame and singe a knife."

"First," said Bagpipe, "I ought to boil water."

"Why?"

He told me. "It's common sense that whenever lead is yanked out of somebody, the real danger ain't of bleeding. It's infection. You first need washing."

"Bag," I said, "you've got a brain."

He chuckled. "Me?"

"You. So attack it. Don't pay a mind to how much I bleed or plead. Your target is a slug. The next thing is for you to extract lead. You seen Mrs. Krickitt perform slug extraction a few times. I have. Bagpipe, don't you faint if it's covered with blood. If there's any swooning, I'll handle it. Got me?"

"Gotcha, Mr. Titus."

Hearing it gave me strength.

Tin Pan became curious, asked what was wrong, and then was told to face forward and resist offering his medical opinion.

A few minutes later, water was boiling, and I could hear a yelping Bagpipe washing his hands in water that no human could endure. Not for himself. For me. When he returned, the sleeves of Bag's work shirt were rolled up into a serious scroll, as though ready to perform a need-be miracle.

"Lucky I tote two little gadgets in my saddlebag."

"So I've heard. Can they slash it out?"

"If you can take misery. At least they're washed."

"Cut me."

"All right." He returned, holding a short spar of silver. "This is a probe. Because first, we locate the bullet; then, we dig to fetch it."

I pulled up yellow. "Perhaps it could wait until Doc Callendor can come to Spur Box, to see what's hit me."

"Maybe," said Bagpipe, "you're sort of lucky. Because I seen that old butcher carve a waddy up into small servings, and it took him half a night to do it. Between you and me, Mr. Titus, I wouldn't allow Doc Callendor to whack a tail off Cleopatra if she'd been dead for a week."

His humor almost made me forget.

"Be right back," Bagpipe said.

He returned with a small flask of colorless liquid;

a libation, I was presuming, that Mr. Hop prohibited near horses, cattle, or firearms.

With his teeth, Bag popped the cork. "Here's to courage," he said with a grin, not offering it me but gulping some for himself. Then it was my turn. "It'll roast your insides," he warned. It did. "That's good liquor," Bagpipe bragged. "Costly. It's what Molly serves at The Bent Ace."

I grunted. "That hooch would peel paint."

Bag tried to look offended. Pulling the bottle from my hand, he knocked back another healthy (or rather unhealthy) gulp. Then a third. "You're right, Mr. Titus. Somebody's been cutting this stuff. It ain't quite up to full potency." He looked at me. "Have another dose?"

"No thanks."

Bag pushed the mouth of the bottle an inch or two closer to my mouth, his face sobering to serious. "Please do it, Mr. Titus." His hand coaxed my shoulder. "You'll turn grateful. Hear?" Understanding, I took a bigger swallow, allowing it to burn itself out inside me, then another. "Lie back," he told me. "I'm going to soap your belly over and around that purple puncture. And be still. You been gut shot. So best you try'n vacation yourself."

Bag dunked his probe in the booze and went to work. He was hurting me some. And then terrible horrible miserable, until I fired off a scream. Pulling my belt out of my jean loops, Bag stuck the leather crosswise in my teeth.

"Bite," he said, "or you'll disturb Tin Pan, which means that maybe all us handsome waddies just might miss out on supper."

I bit. Bagpipe probed into me again. The metal probe was hot from its boiling, which didn't ease me. He final quit, and I spat out my belt.

"Did you get it out?"

"First I gotta find it." He put the leather back in my teeth again and continued his poking. "Found it. Ain't in too deep. Good thing I brung needle-nose pliers. They'll pinch it and pull."

This new pain was twice as hurtful as the probing. Bag's pliers gripped ahold of something inside me, maybe a kidney, and then a few more organs that he figured I didn't necessary need. It had to stop. Had to. Please, had to, yet it kept on close to crazy.

"Dang it, Tee. Quit your bleeding."

After he took the pliers out, I asked, "Did you get it, Bag? I can't take another helping. Feels like you're using a shovel. Tell me you got it."

"No, I didn't get it. You're leaking a bucket of blood. I can't see. All I can do is feel, guess, and then hope whatever ball I yank out is lead."

"Give me . . . another drink of rotgut."

"You'll pass out or die."

I took a swallow. "God, I hope so."

Above me, as I lay on my back, Florida seemed to be swirling and turning. Only a dull hum. I could no longer feel my feet inside my boots. Like going barefoot. In my mouth, the belt tasted salty with sweat, a taste you could smell. Like bad cooking.

"This'll hang some hurt on you, Mr. Titus. I won't pretend to story about it. So hang on, and chew up leather like it was a strip of breakfast bacon."

The pain made me grunt, straining hard, feeling the blood reddening my face, flooding my eyes and brain and reason. It was repeated death, getting killed over and over, and it wouldn't stop. On and on. Bagpipe swore. Not really fancy. Just a talented stream of old favorites, linked together as sausages. One oath after another.

Bagpipe quit cussing.

Eyes closed, I figured the slug was out, and I was starting to regain my breathing. Until Bag poured bad whiskey into the bullet hole in my belly. My world exploded into flame. Beyond pain. And beyond either sanity or consciousness. All went black.

Warm water.

Somebody, who didn't smell like Mrs. Krickitt, was

washing me. My fingers unclenched. A little hunk of metal dropped into my open hand. One crude ball of lead with uneven edges. Bagpipe explained it with a single word.

"Souvenir."

CHAPTER TWENTY

T he wagon kept bumping along.

Somewhere close by, just a few feet east of my head, Tin Pan was cackling some unmerciful melody to Right and Wong. He sang about as sweet as the mules could bray. I lay on my back inside the chucky but not alone; Vinegar was beside me, pressing wads of rag against my sore belly. The cloths were pink. My blood.

"Don't let on to the men," I mumbled.

Vin shook his head. "There's only four of us knowed. Bag, me, Tin Pan, and yourself." He snorted. "Maybe one other.

"Who?"

"She's following this blessed wagon. It's that ugly cussed bonebag we call the Devil's Daughter. Horses do funny at times. Can't explain how come, but that mess of a mustang mare you favor as a mount seems to hanker to tag along. To worry about you."

It hurt to talk. "She's . . . she is a good animal, Vin. Works willing. Daughter helped me with Micah. She seemed to sense something was rotten wrong and didn't desert me in the night."

"Anything you say, Mr. Titus."

"Thanks for that, too."

"You're earning it. Oh, there's been a few grumbles of complaint; you know, as it's sort of a cowpoke's nature to gripe at one stringy bean buried in a heaping hot plate of good ones. But in the overall, the boys might respect you more'n ya cogitate."

"Only if I respect them. And I do. The same way Mr. Hopple did." I sucked a painful breath. "Lordy, Vin, can you believe it all happened?"

"Nope." His voice was gray. "Not hardly."

Pulling the rags off my stomach, Vin felt them, as though assessing my blood loss.

"Don't be alarmed," I said. "It only takes a few spoons of blood to discolor a entire shirt. There's plenty left in me, Vin. My name is MacRobertson. And I'm a hardy Scot."

"You certain be." He pressed more rags to the wound.

"Ah," said Tin Pan, "Titus mending?"

"Yup," Vinegar answered. "He's either too dumb or too dutiful to kick off." He grinned at me. "Oh, in case you actual die, relax afterward. I'll sashay the entire outfit on to Homestead. Most of us know the way."

"How close are we?"

Vinegar nodded. "Be there tomorrow."

Trying to sit up, then aware that there wasn't enough strength for it, I said, "Hey, that's impossible. I know where we are. Sort of."

"Me too. I've made this drive a score of times. More'n you. And believe it, I'm telling you it'll be tomorrow."

"How come?"

"You been dreaming for a couple days. Out of your skull and muttering about a girl and some ghost. I told the boys a fib. Said you caught a fever. So shut that gaping hole under your nose and rest the one in your belly."

I slept. For how long, I never quite knew. But whenever I'd open my eyes, Vinegar was there, trying to feed me or change the stinking pile that constituted a bed. He continued the pressure on my body, resting his tired head on the rags to stop the bleeding.

"It's morning. Where are we?"

"Close, Mr. Titus," said Vin. "Clumping into Homestead."

"Stand me up."

"No. You'll possible drain to death."

"Don't matter, Vinegar. I'm not to ride at Homestead lying in a chucky but on a horse. In front. And in charge."

Vin growled. "You certain inherit a cantanky pinch of Rob Roy inside you somewheres. I'll grant you that."

"Thanks. I'm not ashamed of toting a lick of Eudora, or of Mr. Mac. Like our Spur Box cattle, whatever be natural bred."

Vinegar shrugged. "However you perceive it, Mr. Titus. I'm mere a puncher who don't know a skink from a skunk."

"Vin, please help me to my feet."

With old Vinegar's hands clamped under my armpits, to stand become sudden actual, even though the bullet hole seemed to howl into a holler.

"You okay, Tee? Sorry. I meant Mr. Titus."

With a grin, I told Vinegar that I'd be sound and ripe for new territory.

Vin nodded. "Ain't nothing like the excite of riding a strong horse onto fresh turf. Ground that's never been hoofed. A man's gotta fork across uncustom land to discover his own self." He grinned. "Like you done."

Hearing his wisdom, even though crudely stated, sort of lightened me an ounce. Just as Bagpipe had confessed, days ago, I sudden knew who I was. And better yet, *why*.

"Want me to saddle you a horse, Mr. Titus?"

"No thanks, Vin." I faked a confident smile at him. "I'll grit it out lonesome."

Although it hurt me worse'n a hundred hangovers, I did slap my saddle to Daughter and then occupied it. Vin also mounted. Yet I noticed his hovering around, as though expecting me to fall off and kiss Florida. Three times, I near did.

We made it into town. A distant sign, facing west, announced the receiving center:

HOMESTEAD MEAT CO.

Perhaps, because of the storm of a few days ago, there hadn't been an excess of cattle to process. I noticed the holding pens seemed near to empty. In an open doorway, a tall lanky gentleman who was observing our arrival gestured at me, then walked out from shade into sunlight.

"Morning," he said, saluting by touching his white Panama hat brim with the edge of the cleanest finger that I'd seen in a week. "I'm Jack Dowell."

"Howdy," I said. "My name's MacRobertson. We ranch the Spur Box outfit south of Naples."

"Say," he said, "that's some trip in trouble weather.

165

You gents must about be due recreation." He was selling as well as buying. "After we deal for your cattle, what measure of pleasure y'all cotton to?"

"Had I the energy," I told him, "I'd die."

We bargained on a price. His first offer didn't sound adequate, so as he kept jabbering on about hard times, I pointed at his empty pens and allowed him to notice how I was eyeing another sign. A competitor's.

SOUTHERN PACKING CORP.

When Mr. Dowell sweetened the pot considerable, we shook hands. Our count, instead of five hundred beefs, tallied three head short of four hundred. Considering, it was near magical we'd brought so many so far, and through dreadful.

He paid cash. On an even four hundred head!

My ability to deal pleased me. As I was stuffing the big-denomination bills into my jeans pocket, I stopped to peel off two hundreds. "I'll require a few fives and tens," I told him, "as a bonus for my crew."

He obliged.

"Say," he asked me as the two of us settled money square and shook hands, "don't we usual dicker with an older gentleman by the name of Hopple?"

"Mr. Ornell Hopple passed away during the drive.

He's been foreman since before I got born." Swallowing, I added, "Our top hand."

"Sorry to hear."

"Thanks. We miss him."

It was Micah I missed, an empty hole in me deeper and more hurtful than any slug could puncture.

Twenty minutes later, I donated sawbucks into the hard hands of our punchers. Realizing that before the evening sun had departed, much of their hard-won bonuses would evaporate, never to vacate Homestead. They all thanked me in a polite way. Several glanced at my gut and inquired if I was recovering. Someone had spilled the secret, but now it didn't matter.

Looking at their faces, I sudden knew them for exactly what they be. No less, and no uppity. Just cowhands, dirty, exhausted, glad to be alive and possible even amazed. Each man pulled the sweaty wet leather off the spine of a horse and rubbed the animal dry. They also made certain that our stringers and mules, in pens, had ample oats. Then, final free and whooping, they scampered off toward the center of town, to a place called The Golden Garter. It was, I was presuming, a local answer to The Bent Ace. Homestead and Dry Bone seemed content to ignore the Volstead Act and Prohibition.

Tin Pan, after buying another mule harness and

restocking the chucky, all at my expense, went another direction, in search of a Chinese family who resided in Homestead. Two of our most senior hands, Vinegar and Bagpipe (my nurses), stopped, then took a step toward me. I stood alone.

"You fancy a celebration with us no-goods?" Vinegar wanted to know.

Bag added, "We'd be honored."

I grinned. "Thanks, but I have plans."

They waved.

Off they hurried in a beeline to The Golden Garter, impatient to get drunk, sick, robbed, or fisted. Standing there, almost as a concerned parent, I watched them disappear. No matter how tender you care about people, I was discovering, you'll not alter anyone. Best afford them the noblest gift that a man can offer his neighbor.

Acceptance.

CHAPTER TWENTY-ONE

I missed out on The Golden Garter.

Not because of my disapproval, or the fact that I was a MacRobertson snob; but only due to being barely able to stand without my knees jacking, or keeling over. After slowly gimping toward the center of town, I spotted salvation and its shingle of welcome:

MRS. SUTTER'S BOARDING

It was where Micah had said the two of us would stay. Soon as my knuckles knocked, she answered, with a motherly face, thick body, and sensible shoes.

"I'm Vanilla Sutter. Can I help you?"

Pulling off a filthy hat, I said, "The name's MacRobertson. Our outfit just pushed in four hundred head. If you please, I'd like to buy a bath, a bed, and tomorrow's breakfast. As long as it isn't *beef*. I'll pay up front."

Pointing at a bolted-down bootjack on the stoop, she said, "Yank off your boots, leave 'em, and march yourself around to the rear."

"Why?"

"That's where the tub is. Under a shed roof. You'll find clean towels, soap, and a generous tank of hot water." She eyed my filthy clothes. "Toss the duds over a white wall. By time you wake up, they'll be scrubbed and dried. But keep your personals on you."

Seeing as there was a smart of Mrs. Krickitt to her, I didn't argue and would do exact as she'd ordained.

"You'll find a purple bathrobe handy, at the tub, to wear up the back stairs to your bedroom. Number Nine. Leave the robe on a peg outside the door. For the next bather."

"Thanks."

"It'll be ten dollars, in advance. Breakfast is free. Served hot and plentiful at six o'clock every morning. Agreeable?" I paid her. "Hannibal, he's my helper, will see to them sorrowful boots. Lick a shine at 'em. If wore through, he'll cobble. So rest peaceful."

I grinned at her. "Is this Heaven?"

Mrs. Sutter chuckled. "Not quite. You got a hefty load of living to burden before you greet Heaven, or it you. As you been blessed with manners, young man, I reckon you'll make it up yonder." Again she eyed my clothes. "Hope you do, son. From the grubby look in your eyes, you've already ate a helping of Hell."

The tub was sort of old greeny tin. Like at home.

Water hot, soap smelled good, and I had to fight sleep once my body was soaking. There was even a clean sponge. Later, a white towel felt thick, soft, and had been slightly scented with lilac.

Upstairs, I left the robe on a peg.

Clean sheets, a plump but yielding pillow. Naked, I lay there, alone in a divine place called Number Nine, almost praying that I'd never have to leave here and could abide forever. As I lay on my back, my head was sinking deeper into the cream-colored muslin pillowcase, until it smothered both my ears.

My eyes closed.

Though alone in Number Nine's cozy comforts, the Cowboy Ghost was also there. Like me, too pooped to palaver. His silence approved our drive to Homestead.

Anytime I'm beat-up exhausted, I get giddy, as if life's nothing but some silly joke.

Memory hauled me back to high school English and a teacher I enjoyed. Miss Bonham had requested our being creative, even comical, and compose a loving encounter between Romeo and Juliet. "They might be," she said, "running across a meadow of daisies, arms extended, eager to entwine." As she liked what I'd submitted, I had to stand and share my wit with the class.

I first explained that the scene was a torrid romance as it would have been written by our math teacher, Mr. Orvis Glumgartig, who had the sense of humor of a fire hydrant:

Were our star-crossed lovers 100 kilometers apart, and Juliet skipped out of Padua at 3:35 PM, traveling at a brisk trot of 15 miles per hour, while Romeo (on horseback) split from Genoa at 4:05 at 300 MPH, how long would it take Juliet to be totally trampled?

Prior to impact, I slept.

In the night I awoke only once; it happened by rolling over and pestering the bullet hole. After a brief wonder where I was, sleep repossessed me. A bell sounded. Not loud, but proudly persistent, as if the bell ringer had just invented dawn.

"Breakfast!" I heard Mrs. Sutter say. "Final call."

My clothes and shined boots were outside the door of Number Nine, neatly arranged. So, with clenched teeth, I managed to climb inside everything, then hobble down the carpeted stairs.

"Good morning, Mrs. Sutter."

"Morning to you, Mr. MacRobertson." In an apron, a spatula in her hand, she asked, "How do your prefer your hen fruit, and how many? You didn't git a supper."

Hunger bit me, the awareness that I'd had nothing to eat in days except for a couple of oranges. "Six, please. Any way you fry or scramble will be perfect." I wasn't up to major decisions.

"Ham or bacon?"

"Ham."

"You like grits?"

I grinned. "Doesn't everyone? Yes, please, I certain do, if they're hot buttered, with just a sprinkle of nutmeg."

"Coming up."

While waiting, it struck me that this would be one of many breakfasts without Micah. My emptiness wasn't hunger for food but a longing for a massive man whose smile had cracked open every morning into a fresh egg.

A plate arrived in two minutes, exactly as ordered, with two thick buttermilk biscuits for good measure. Plus orange juice. When I was fixing to leave, Vanilla Sutter looked me up and down again, now approvingly.

"Hard to believe"—she shook her head—"you're the sorry disaster who arrived here yesterday. What happened? Did the diggers drag you across the flats behind runaway horses? No matter. Hope we made you welcome."

"Yes'm. Thank you, Mrs. Sutter. Believe me, I'll return a year from now. So have Number Nine ready. And please, more of those biscuits."

"You seem on the young side, you know, here to your lonesome. Where's all your drovers?"

I shrugged. "Something about a garter. And, right prompt, it's time I cumulated them to head home."

Mrs. Sutter made a face. "The Golden Garter. That so-called establishment would offend Lucifer hisself. Behind it, there's a run-down place that rents beds. No sheets, but plenty of lice. The *lady* in charge gets six bits a flop. And were I a gambler, I'd wager that's where you'll locate the poor corpses. It's called Bedbug Paradise."

"I'll go there."

"Oh, and next door, there's a unwashed dentist that yanks out busted teeth, stitches cuts, extracts broken glass, applies antiseptic or bandages. And sells crutches."

For some reason, a sudden memory of Mrs. Emma Krickitt. My nose could smell her iodine, and my flesh cringed at her needle. Why did I miss her so much? Well, at least for today I'd enjoyed a benevolent breakfast served by a spanking-clean lady whose name was a flavor. Vanilla.

"Thank you again, Mrs. Sutter." I put my hat on. "Guess I ought to be trailing on out of here. Northwest."

"Come back."

Waving, I said, "Count on it."

It took most of the morning to assemble every meandering member of our Spur Box crowd. And to count their swollen, booze-broken faces.

Spider Schellenberger, his split lips reddened by lipstick, couldn't walk and therefore had to be carried, by Hoofrot, Bug Eye, and Spout. Vinegar was barely able to stand. And as it hurt to open his eyes in daylight, he had to be guided toward our wagons by Domino. Dom's thumb had been broken. I considered it wisest not to ask how, or why, leaving all of my punchers to crawl from The Golden Garter with sweet recollections of their own making, those of pleasure, and those of pain.

Organizing them, in order to point toward Spur Box, was about all that Tin Pan and I could muster. Even without a bullet hole that still hurt worse'n holy.

Father's philosophy was echoing in my ear: "A rancher," he'd told me, "don't hire on a genius to do cowhanding. Mostly they're a mess of simple men."

We headed west.

Tin Pan drove the chucky. Before leaving Homestead, I told Tin to make certain that all horses and mules were fed generous portions of oats, which they relished. Oats, as Ornell Hopple remarked, would retain them loyal to us and following along for more.

Though hurting, I rode drag. Alone. Here, at the tail of our cowless procession, I could gather up a poke who tumbled out of his saddle.

Several did, to smack Florida.

CHAPTER TWENTY-TWO

Days later, we found, righted, and repaired the tool wagon. The jolt of approaching my brother's grave wasn't easy.

Now, however, was not a moment for mourning. On the way home, I had time to ponder, remembering so many of the positive lessons that Micah had taught. It had taken years to harken and heed the depth of his judgment and versatility. Micah Samson MacRobertson, my brother: the lion who was spiritually a lamb.

"Keep a journal," he'd advised. "It's more'n a diary that mere records events. Your journal probes personality, to recall how a man settles a problem. And more important, about people. That's what a life is, Titus. Just a collection of critters you touch and who have touched you. Flowers or weeds."

"You mean like Greer O'Ginty?" I'd asked him, still

disturbed about that fateful Sunday afternoon, a day when I was seven and Micah was pounded to the ground.

My brother had nodded.

"Yes, even about the times you've taken the drub of defeat. Remember, young brother, and learn thereby."

I hadn't yet kept a log.

Yet if ever, one observation of the moment would certain get jotted in capital letters and would read as follows: Whenever unencumbered by cows and pointed toward *home*, the mules, men, and horses do fashion smartly along at a frisky gait. The animals knew. Spurs weren't necessary for Spur Box.

In five days, a few hours less, we loped across the boundary line, wagons and all, and onto our belonging range.

"Yahoo," mumbled Vinegar's shaggy voice.

His empty cheer fell chilly and silent. The other cowhands realized that today wasn't a ordinary homecoming; we'd come back without Micah and minus Mr. Hop. For years, summer upon summer, I recalled as we cantered closer, I'd witnessed our punchers returning at a hat-whacker gallop from a cattle drive, full of Perdition, itching to hoot mischief. Bug Eye would honk his harmonica so that Spider could sweep Mrs. Krickitt into his whippy arms and then waltz her to the tune.

She always complied with a curtsy.

Looking back a century ago when I was still a child, moments such as these somehow welded us all together into a common clan. Not fancy. Just an isolated brigade to survive on a scorching Florida flat and do neighborly, people who cared about one another so deep that it was pap to profess it outright.

Home meant Spur Box.

We lived here.

We'd arrived. Not with tradition. Because we came bearing sorry news, twice over. From a corner of my eye, I noticed the punchers studying me; they were knowing that the trial of telling the stay-behinds now fell to the youngest among us. The beardless boy who'd recently been knighted Mr. Titus.

There they stood together: two of them, in front of our white house, assessing us. The lean one waved and the large one saluted.

Father and Mrs. Krickitt.

As we rode closer, I could almost read the anxiety in the eyes of our two seniors. Silently they counted riders, no doubt coming up short and wondering the where-abouts of key individuals. Our hands reined, we dis-mounted, then pulled wet saddles off tired animals to rub them dry, treat 'em to oats, and then gently spank their rumps toward an open meadow of fresh, familiar grass, plus a welcoming taste of home water.

Trying to climb down with dignity, I faltered unstable. No anchor to station me still. As I was fixing to fall, Father caught me.

"That storm last week," he said, "was a ripsnorter. So we're grateful y'all are back." His voice couldn't mask concern.

"Not all," I told him. "Only those you see."

Father's eyes flicked busy, glancing first one direction and then another, wordless searching for a large son. And a top hand. Men like Micah and Ornell, although opposites in physical composition, don't stumble along too often. When they do, the outfit that harbors them shines blessed.

They didn't ask. Because they couldn't bear to.

Mr. Mac and Mrs. Krickitt simply stood their ground, already understanding, having experienced the returns from decades of cattle drives, when not every drover came home. The brace of them were Florida cattle ranchers, fierce as the earth they commanded, and had witnessed more'n one tragic absence. Emma and Rob Roy had outlived ordinary: The years had tanned them to leather, a braid of durable ribbons to guide the rest of us along a course of continuity. Reins to reason.

Without inquiring, they both knew.

Neither of them would consider undignifying our feelings by premature probes. Their eyes looked ready to help us shoulder a coffin. For this bit of domestic diplomacy, I felt a craving to hold them close to me, only for a moment. Yet I resisted.

Facing them, as they waited to learn the details of death, made me realize my upcoming task. So briefly I told them the straight of it. Nodding, they accepted the truth, knowing that Ornell Hopple had lived a full, respected life. He'd lived among cows and died among them. Micah, however, was only twenty-nine.

Walking slow between them, toward the house, there was much I was aching to share. Tons of toting. Heavier than a heart could hold. Yet fatigue was excusing me, momentarily, from my ominous obligation. Around me, I was feeling the stanchion of Father's mighty arms, supporting me, then steering me toward our house.

"We pushed four hundred head," I told him, "the entire way to Homestead after we were hit by the Seminole, then by a awesome storm. But the Indians didn't try to kill any of us. Just cattle, and only in defiance. Had they wanted to, the Seminole could've poked arrows through every manjack. But they were there, unseen, hissing a arrow anywhere they cottoned." Looking at Father, I said, "Thanks for stowing the guns with Tin Pan. We used 'em to spook cowdiggers."

We sat, three of us, at our kitchen table. The pair of elders had nothing to say, but merely eyeballed me as though I'd come to them bearing secrets from Saturn.

Mrs. Krickitt, who couldn't abide a man sitting without food before him, sudden was up, to warm pie at the stove. Inhaling all of her crisp and spicy goodness brought me home.

"Here," I said to Father, unpocketing a rumpled roll of cash, "is what's currently paid in Homestead. Some's missing. I gave the hands a ten-dollar bonus. Tomorrow, another fin. Because I promised. A MacRobertson's word is signed and solid. We were shorthanded and they earned it. Besides, we don't have Mr. Hopple to pay anymore."

In a surprisingly calm tone, Father asked who promoted me in charge of our cattle drive.

"Mother Nature. I now happen to be your only son. If you can't savvy your allegiance to me, please be aware, Father, that I understand mine to Spur Box. What's more, sir, your second son undertakes." Staring at him, I added, "I can cut it."

"Tell me . . . please, tell us more about him."

"After I'm rested. For now, better know that Micah

wasn't another Rob Roy, as you desired."

"Micah was mine. My boy."

"Pardon me, Father, but you're slight mistaken on that score. Although I never knew Mother, I do know my brother better than either of you. And, in many ways, Micah was *her* son. More than yours. You wanted a competent heir? Your wish is granted. Here I squat."

"You?" His one word was an odd combining of dismay and a newborn awe.

"Hear him out," Mrs. Krickitt warned him. "He's growed." Without another word, she placed a fork and a slab of warm rhubarb pie before me, plus a white mug of hot tea with a wedge of lemon.

"Micah and I," I informed my father, "were opposites. Like the two masks of drama. I am comedy. Micah was tragedy, one of family forging. He didn't want to be buried here at Spur Box. His final wish was to die free."

Father's face seemed to freeze. "So be it," he whispered. "Yet what you've told me, Titus, is difficult to accept. So maverick to what I've always believed and carried as a banner."

"I've known my brother sixteen years, and he wasn't a second *you*. In truth, he was his mother's child, Eudora Mae's."

Father said, "I suspected Micah was hers."

"Believe it, sir. In death, Micah became his own man."

"And with his death, Titus Timothy," my father said to me in a surprisingly soft voice, "you became yours."

CHAPTER TWENTY-THREE

Y ou're bleeding!" Mrs. Krickitt said in alarm.
As my hand touched soiled clothes, I felt a warm
wetness, plus the unmistakable sickening-sweet
stench of stale blood. "It's all right," I told her with a
forced grin. "A bullet hole doesn't beg stitching."

Her hand felt my forehead. "You are feverish, boy.
Fixing to burst into flame." Perhaps knowing that I
wanted her tending, Mrs. Krickitt loosened my shirt and
belt.

"He stopped one," Father said in a whisper.

"Is it still inside you?" she asked.

"No." Reaching into the tiny watch pocket of my
denims, I produced a little lead souvenir and tossed it on
the kitchen table.

"Who pulled it?" Father asked me.

"Bagpipe. Prior to, he made me swallow some of his

Bent Ace elixir, stilled in Dry Bone, with a flavor that would gag a maggot. Then he probed into me, located the slug, and extracted it with his needle-nosers."

"Holy cow!" My father bent closer to study my purple crater. "Bagpipe dug quite a pit into you."

As I was describing a few more crimsony details, Mrs. Krickitt moved to the sink cabinet and returned with clean rags, and armed with a bottle of carbolic.

"Please," I said, "not that stuff. It'll burn me to ashes."

"Titus. I fully intend to dilute it. But we ought to bathe your outside because of that runny wound. The bullet might have grazed your spleen. Full of blood vessels and will bleed like all fury."

In school, we'd learned something about the human spleen: a blood filter to remove older red and white blood cells so that the fresher cells perform better. It wasn't surprising that Mrs. Krickitt knew physiology. She read a lot. So, deciding not to kick up a fuss, I allowed her to attend me. Perhaps she'd be a bit more professional than Bag or Vin.

I told them how Vinegar Swinton had kept on blotting my gut with bloody rags, hour after hour.

"He done proper," she said. "The pressure he applied helped stem the internal bleeding, to clot it. Vin knows more than he lets on. Add to that, you got powerful lucky, dodging both infection and hemorrhage. A wonder you made it home. How long ago did you get gunshot? Yesterday? Day before?"

"A week ago."

"No."

I nodded. "Diggers threatened us on the route to Homestead. In fact, I did business dealing with the packing company in sorry shape. If we didn't bargain steep enough, I apologize. Next drive, I'll be one year older and a decade smarter."

"Titus," my father told me, "you done noble."

"Please steady him, Mr. Mac. This carbolic rinse is going to sting. But it'll be better than a dirty hole. Or infected scab."

Father held me. It took a plenty of him because the carbolic, even diluted, burned like insanity. A lance cut through me. I didn't scream. Just struggled and strained against my father's purchase until Mrs. Krickitt quit laundering. The agony faded. But not once did I holler.

"You have fortitude," my father told me as he wiped the sweat off my face. "Did it burn you frightful?"

"It got my attention."

"Ought go upstairs," Father said, "and sleep yourself whole. You right bloody earned a rest."

"He's right," Mrs. Krickitt added. "And you know how I dislike admitting it. Stand up, Titus, and we'll support you to your bedroom."

"No need," my father said.

With a sudden heft of his arms, he lifted me like a rag doll. Then, with a gentleness I never knew he had, Mr. Mac carried his only surviving relative up the stairs. Eyes closed, I heard the pointed toes of heavy cowboy boots kicking the risers, all the way up. I liked the rough smell and feel of his shirt against my face. This was the closest I'd ever been to him. Or he to me. I wanted him to carry me forever. But we'd reached the upstairs hall.

He stopped. Then, for a fleeting moment, he clutched me closer to him and lightly kissed my hair. My imagination? Such a gesture just wasn't Mr. Mac's style. Yet I was praying it was true. Until now, in my entire life, nobody in my family had ever kissed me. Not even once. Without thinking, I pressed my head against my father's shirt, wanting to remain tucked in his arms.

"Please," I asked him, "instead of my own room, tote me to Micah's. So I can sleep in my brother's bed."

"Done."

Laying me down on Micah's checkerboard quilt, he pulled off my boots. "Before you fill this'n here double," he said, "eat regular and prosper a few pounds."

"In time. I'm just sixteen. Micah was twenty-nine. So measure me again thirteen years from today. I believe, sir, you might be amazed."

He almost grinned. "Already am."

"Thanks."

"Before I go down to the bunkhouse, like usual, and welcome home the hands, is there anything you require, Titus? If so, I'll fetch it personal."

"One thing."

"Well?"

"It's a book, sort of. Micah kept it underneath the bed. He called it his journal. As I fall asleep, I'll take a bit of my brother along."

Bending, he grunted, then located a book that partly split open in his clumsy fingers. Before surrendering it, the thick bare-knuckle fighter's hands briefly caressed it.

"This it?"

Nodding as I noticed the bulky handwriting, I said, "Yes, I believe so. He'd honest want me to have it. Thank you, Father."

As he handed over the journal, his large paw brushed my small one, lingering for only a second or two, then pulled away. For a long moment Father observed me, perhaps wondering who I was, or rather who I'd sudden sprouted to be, and how come we had never quite been introduced.

"Rest," he said. A hard hand touched my cheek. With no further words to spare, he turned to abandon Micah's bedroom, his boot heels punishing the stairs. Between thumps, I heard a tinkling jingle of the rowel wheels on his spurs.

Although exhausted and still sizzling from Mrs. Krickitt's carbolic rinse, I opened my brother's journal. It was a lifetime log of a boy and then a young man. Intimate thoughts about common occurrences. The very first one, in particular, captured my heart. A young child had printed:

Today I picked a little yellow flower from our meadow to take to Mother. But it never reached her. Father took it from me. Then taught me how to fold my fingers to a fist.

The open journal fell to my chest.

"Yup," I heard those long-ago insensitive voices bellowing, "that Micah is a bull of a boy. A natural boxer. He's going to be a second Rob Roy."

They didn't know. None of them knew. Except for maybe Mrs. Krickitt, and me. Father was mere one more member of the hooting crowd, beneath hats in the air, lusting for Sunday sporting. Satanic entertainment. My own fists clenched. How I almost hated Micah for going along with it, for yielding to all of their primitive lust to watch and wager on pain. So they fed their gusto. Squeezed the blood, drop by drop, from the soft yellow petals of a meadow's bloom, hammering a mindless spike through the palm of a innocent child.

Again I studied Micah's book.

Before rolling over and surrendering to sleep, I felt compelled to see his last entry, written a day prior to our departing from Spur Box on the cattle drive. The date told me I guessed right. It was a sonnet:

Brothers

I am my brother's brother. No surprise
That I'd make near to twice of him, in size.
His name is Titus, and I'll ride beside
My brother, Titus Timothy, with pride.

The twain of us are not alike. You see,
He'll maybe try to be another me.
I pray that he will not! I know he can
Become a rancher all himself. A man.

He'll wish to fly, to soar, to distance roam
Before he finds himself. Right here at home.
And so to nourish him to strong and tall,
I serve beside young Titus, as a wall.

I stand between them, stoically and still,
To spare my brother from my father's will.

Closing the journal, cradling it beneath my chin with both of my arms, I lay on my side, my cheek on Micah's pillow. His smell was a strong animal scent. My brother's nearness blanketed me. A comfortable feeling.

Two or three days ago, passing by Micah's grave on our return to Spur Box, our family's history became more clear. Rob Roy had once been a child, one probable molded and hardened by his resolute sire, Maxwelton Ramsay MacRobertson. Thus it became obvious how to honor my dead brother with a simple gift. Do something he couldn't do:

I'd forgive Father.

Closing my eyes, resisting tears, I realized that the presence with me now was entirely Micah. There no longer seemed to be much of a Cowboy Ghost, and I'd be associating less and less with him. Yet I still wondered who he was.

"Cowboy Ghost, are you Micah?"

No, not at all, deliberation told me. But then, snug in my brother's bed, the true identity of this mystical spirit slowly unfolded. Oddly enough, the Cowboy Ghost was nobody in my past. Instead, he was the fortune of my future.

"You," I said, "are the man I will someday be."

CHAPTER TWENTY-FOUR

My eyes opened.

The bedroom was dark, yet a faint shard of late moonlight sifted through the open window, illuminating Micah's clock.

"Ten minutes to five."

Forcing myself out of bed was no picnic, yet I hacked it, pulling on boots and cussing at Mrs. Krickitt's infernal (and supposedly diluted) carbolic acid. My teeth were grinding an entire way down the stairs and through an unlit kitchen.

No sign of Father, our housekeeper, or even Cleopatra.

Outside, I walked with starchy resolution to the bunkhouse. No lights. Plenty of snoring. Tin Pan was still asleep. So were the punchers, every one, no doubt assuming that because Mr. Hop wasn't around, they'd dog it lazy a extra hour. Right?

"Wong," as Tin would say.

Using a cook spoon and a skillet, I bonged a jolting good morning, loud enough to roust all Florida and parts of Cuba.

"Up," I shouted. "First off, tidy this bunkhouse before it resembles the Dry Bone dump. It ain't Sunday, boys. Tin Pan, please favor us by cranking up your cookery, chop chop, or else I'll summon Mrs. Krickitt down here to paint you proper."

"I sure up, Mr. Titus," our cook answered, adding a dash of Chinese to flavor his disposition. Tin's thumb flicked a match to kerosene.

In a breath, I witnessed every blessed cowpoke roll out in dazed disbelief: Vinegar . . . Spout . . . Bug Eye . . . Domino . . . Fitch . . . Horrible . . . Spider . . . Bagpipe . . . Hoofrot . . . Jilly . . . Fat Cat . . . Shorty . . . reaching for the wrong boot, complaining, and guessing aloud what Tin Pan would burn for breakfast. One by ugly one, sleep-swollen faces stared at their honcho like morning lanterns that individually brighten all over town. They assessed me, knew I meant business, and hustled.

"I gotcha, Mr. Titus," mumbled Vinegar.

While Tin was dressing, I stirred up his stove.

Though hankering to, I didn't eat with the hands. Allowing them their privacy, I returned to our kitchen to greet Mrs. Krickitt at the massive black Acme American six-griddle, and Mr. Mac, already drumming the table with hungry fingers.

"Father." I nodded to him. "Good morning, Mrs. Krickitt. Please fry me three over easy, some bacon, grits, a couple of hot biscuits, and coffee black."

"No glass of milk?" she asked me.

"Not today. Maybe I'll sneak a drop in the coffee. To remind myself that I'm still a kid."

"As you like it. Have a seat."

"Thank you." Pulling out a chair, I sat across the table from Father, eyeing him with a restrained confidence. "By the way," I said, "and with your blessing, sir, I'd like to upgrade Vinegar Swinton to foreman. He deserves top. Domino helps keep him sane on Saturday nights in town. All of our hands respect Vin, he knows the ranch from supper to Sunday, and he'll do us worthy. Until he allows he's wore through at the heel and fixing to retire, and let Bagpipe fill his boots. After that, Fitch."

"Raise in wages?" Father asked.

"If you approve. Not what Mr. Hopple earned, but more'n a dollar a day. Forty a month, a bonus if we profit."

To my surprise, Mr. Mac agreed.

"Another thing," I said, "with Micah gone, we'll need a smith. A day every week. Fatimo Catalina, better known as Fat Cat, knows a Mex in Dry Bone who'll oblige us, and shoe hot. Our east gate's hung shoddy. Storm damage. I'm shipping Horrible and Hoofrot out there with a ladder and tools. We can't allow Spur Box to be poorly represented by a saggy arch."

"What about school?" he asked. Then with a slight smile, added. "I don't mean for Horrible or Hoof. For you."

"I graduated this summer, 'twixt here and Homestead. If you cotton to admire my diploma, you first got to yank up my shirt. I can't frame a lead bullet to gussy up my wall. But I surefire logged a lot of learning. If you doubt my passing marks, go out yonder to the bunkhouse and consult the faculty."

As we whacked into breakfast, Father slurped coffee. A sign of his annoyance. "You don't," he asked me, "fix to manage Spur Box by your lonesome, do you?"

"No, sir, I do not. You and Mrs. Krickitt will please educate, advise, and guide me, so we can continue to work our ranch prosperous. Oh, and I don't intend to reside here solitary. I eventual plan to court Miss Phoebe Ann Quinton, hoping she'll be the next Mrs. Mac." I grinned. "If that's jake with you folks."

"Biddiford's daughter? That rangy-legged Quinton girl?" Father squinted at me. "Used to be pollywogged with freckles. Why that'n?"

"Because I ache for her so bad that my hair hurts. She fills me up and grows me tall. I want Phoebe in my heart and in my home. She also has ranching sense. Besides"—I looked down at my boots—"Phoebe Ann happens to be the only gal I ever notice. Even when she's not around."

Father nodded. "Then maybe you best throw a rope to her neck and brand her a MacRobertson." He stood, carried his plate to the sink, and started to leave. Then turned to study me. "But can she box?"

He left with a straight face.

Our housekeeper poured more coffee. "Well," she said, "I can't speak for Phoebe, but you certain got *himself* hooked." She winked at me. "But go easy, Titus, and reel him in slow. That old longhorn's a bale of barbed wire." She nodded thoughtfully. "He might melt a bit when I offer my land parcel to you and Miss Phoebe, as a wedding present."

"Thank you! Thanks a whole bunch. By the way, are you happy about all this, Miz Emma?" I asked, using her front name for a very first time.

"Nifty news. You're hardier than we imagined. And Mr. Mac, I reckon he's a pound lighter inside than he lets on." She mussed my hair. Then, as she bent down to my face for only a instant, she cautioned, "A hard-boiled egg can hide a soft center. Your pa did, for years. So make certain you never distance your softness from Phoebe's."

I touched her hand. "I promise."

While my father was upstairs, I told Mrs. Krickitt about Micah's death and burial, then about Ornell Hopple. None of it was easy to say, or hear. She didn't cry. For that I was grateful; had she broken down, I might have crumpled. Yet for several minutes Emma Krickitt stared out of her sink window, which looks to our blacksmithy.

A hour later, as Father and I were inspecting the two drive wagons, I told him about my brother and our foreman. Listening, his face froze to ice. He said nothing. Yet I could feel his trembling and read the shattering hurt in his eyes. He shed no tears. The loss of a son and a trusted friend cut beyond grief.

"Next year," I told him, "if your heart's up to better, perhaps we might saddle Highlander and Daughter, to do our next cattle drive together. I'll remember where Micah's buried. You, me, some of the hands could stop there to say words at his grave. And Mr. Hop's. In my Bible, there's a passage from the Book of Micah that I intend to read. About a sword and plowshare."

"Yes," he said, "we ought, Titus. My heart needs such. We truly should do exactly so. For them. And for us."

We left the wagon shed.

As we stood outside our corral, looking west, I

pointed at our barns. "We need a new design," I said. "Everything's too cramped. If it's all right by you, we could expand the tackroom so it's orderly, instead of tangled leather. And enlarge Tin's kitchen. With a set of new knives he'll carve up better grub, and we'll glean more work from the pokes."

"An investment?"

"Yes, sir. One in Spur Box and also in Tin Pan. During the drive, I got to know Tin, and he's a wonder at feeding folks. Not a biscuit short of a miracle. He deserves a raise in pay." I paused. "In Homestead, he and I didn't go Hellbent for The Golden Garter saloon. Next morning, we two were the only ones sober and fit to travel. So an expanded cookery will be Tin's bonus. Not charity. But sound business."

Father studied me. "Is this *you*, Titus?"

"No other." I bent him a grin. "Remember what you can teach me to be, Father. Not a second Rob Roy, just the first Titus Timothy. A young rancher who still got plenty to learn."

Shaking his head, Mr. Mac chuckled some. But then, before I could duck, he hauled off to sock my bicep, a shocker of a right for an aging white-haired boxer. For some reason, by the way he pounded me, it didn't hurt a lick. Even if it had, I certain wouldn't admit it. Or hit him back.

"You're a lot more sturdy," he told me. "A rock."

"So be careful," I warned him, "or you'll break your fist."

Resting a beefy paw lightly on my shoulder, he fought off a broad grin, and lost. "By dang," he said hoarsely, "I got myself a *son*."

About the Author

Robert Newton Peck has written more than sixty books, for adults and youngsters. Raised on a farm, he is familiar with cattle, hogs, and horses. He and a partner own eleven mustangs. Rob now lives in Longwood, Florida, exalts the South, and is rapturously wed. His wife, Sam, is the granddaughter of Robert E. Lee Youngblood.